A DUKE'S WILD KISS

KISS THE WALLFLOWER, BOOK 5

TAMARA GILL

COPYRIGHT

A Duke's Wild Kiss
Kiss the Wallflower, Book 5
Copyright © 2020 by Tamara Gill
Cover Art by Wicked Smart Designs
Editor Grace Bradley Editing
All rights reserved.

ISBN: 978-0-6489312-7-0

DEDICATION

To my dear readers. Thank you for your continual support.

CHAPTER 1

Kent 1810

"ill you do it for me, Hamlyn? We're not far from Chidding Hall, and I need your assurance you will support me with this matter. I need to have your promise, as my friend, that you will help me."

Jasper Abraham, Duke Hamlyn, gaped at his friend, Marquess Oglemoore. Had the fellow gone mad! He shook his head as the blood rushed back into his brain. "Absolutely not. Should I court Miss Quinton, she'd believe me to be enamored of her and possibly want a declaration of love and marriage soon after. If you led her to believe you liked her in town last Season and you did not, then you need to be the one who cleans up after your mistakes. I will not do it for you."

"You owe me, Hamlyn. Did I not step in at Bath just last month and stop those laborers from giving you a good thrashing? Which, by the way, I'm still unsure that you did not deserve."

"Now see here, how is it my fault that one of the men's sweethearts worked at the tavern and rented out her assets to those who could pay? I did not know she was betrothed."

"So you *did* sleep with her? I should have let them thrash you," Oglemoore said, raising his brow with a sarcastic tilt.

"I did no such thing. The woman seized my hand and placed it on her breast at the very moment her betrothed walked into the taproom. Had it been a bout of one-on-one, I would have had no qualms in thrashing the fool for allowing himself to be played so, but one on five and I drew the line." Jasper glared at his friend, disappointed. "What is more surprising to me is your seeking repayment of that service. I should have taken the bloodied nose and been done with it. I do not want to fool Miss Quinton in such a deceitful way. When she was in town last year, what I remember of her was a sweet, pleasant-looking woman. Are you sure you do not wish to court her instead of this Lady Athol Scott chit?"

"Absolutely certain. Miss Quinton is not for me. She's the niece of a duke, granddaughter of one, but other than the house she inherited from her father, and a notable portion, she has little else. Her cousin Lady Clara rules London society like the strict headmaster we had at Eton, and I'm not looking to be under her rule for the remainder of my days.

"I'm Marquess Oglemoore, my family has always married well. Lady Athol owns half of the Scottish lowlands. Imagine the hunting we can do if I marry her. No, Athol suits me very well."

"So, it's a love match, then?" Jasper said, his tone riddled with sarcasm.

Oglemoore's lips thinned into a disapproving line. "I do not love her, but I'm sure that will follow in time. I am fond of the chit, and so she will be my wife. But as for Miss Quinton, you must be the one to show more interest in her person. I need you to do this, truly. When she finds out that I'm courting someone else, she'll be right grieved. But if you, my handsome, English-titled friend show her there is more in the world than me, then she'll move on quick enough."

"And if she chooses me to be the man that she moves on with, what shall I do then? I do not want to be saddled with a wife. I have a mistress in town. A life." The horror of doing such a thing to an innocent woman did not sit well with Jasper, no matter who he had waiting for him back in London. He hated lies and deceit above most things. Oglemoore ought to know better. That he did not was no act of a gentleman.

"Please, my old friend. I'm begging you."

Jasper sighed, glaring across the carriage as it turned through the gates of Chidding Hall. "Very well, but this more than pays back my debt and then some. You owe me by quite a lot."

Oglemoore beamed, clapping his legs with his hands. "I knew I could count on you, my good friend. I shall gladly pay you back tenfold for this. Thank you."

Jasper wasn't so sure he would ever be repaid for acting the lovesick fool trying to turn a woman's eye toward him and off another. Even so, he would do it for his friend since he seemed so desperate. He could be Miss Quinton's friend, guide her away. There need not be anything romantic between them. If he followed that rule, all would be well and work out in the end.

"We're here," Oglemoore said, sliding toward the door.

Jasper picked up his top hat, slapping it onto his head. "Let the games begin," he said, throwing his friend a small grimace.

Let the games begin indeed.

. . .

*O*livia swallowed the bile that rose in her throat at hearing her closest friend declare that she hoped to marry Elliott Keating, Marquess Oglemoore.

"We were introduced at a ball in London. He's affable, and I enjoyed his company. I look forward to seeing him attend the house party," Athol said, a small smile playing about her lips.

The world spun around Olivia, and she clasped her stomach, taking a deep breath to try to stop her stomach contents from making an appearance.

"I had no idea you were even acquainted?" she stated, quite shocked by the fact. Lord Oglemoore was not only one of the most highly placed gentlemen in the *ton*, but he was also one of the most handsome. There was not a feminine heart in London that did not flutter in his presence.

Last Season Olivia had happened upon Lord Oglemoore as he'd stumbled out of the supper room after slipping on some barberry ices. She had awkwardly caught him, but instead of acting the assaulted debutante, she had laughed off the collision, and they had been friends ever since.

"Oh, it's all a bit of a shock to me too. We met at Almacks one Wednesday evening. He asked me to dance, and I agreed. I like him, and I do believe he likes me as well. Or," her friend said, biting her lip, "I hope he does, at least. The ladies speak highly of him, and he seems determined to find a wife. I merely hope he chooses me."

"Of course," Olivia said, her mind reeling. "As a gentleman, I'm sure he will not play you false. If he's shown an interest in you and you return favorably, this house party may end with a betrothal announcement." Olivia smiled at her friend, whom she loved most dearly, but the idea that the one gentleman whom she'd believed to have wanted to court her was instead seemingly interested in Athol was indeed a bitter pill to swallow. How had she been so wrong to read his character and interest so incorrectly?

Athol chuckled. "I do hope so. I seem to have pinned all my hopes on him, even though I have many gentlemen in town who stated they were awaiting my return. But I like Lord Oglemoore best of them all. He will do for me, I believe."

Olivia stared at Athol, unsure what she was hearing was true. Athol was going to marry a man simply because of what? "I'm sorry, my dear, but why marry him if you only think him your best choice? Why not take your time? This is only your second Season. Find a gentleman who puts your heart in his hand and never lets it go."

Her friend shrugged, plopping a grape in her mouth. They were seated out on the terrace that overlooked the grounds of her cousin's estate, the day warm without a breath of wind in the air.

"If you haven't noticed, we are getting rather long in the tooth, Olivia dear. We're both from respectable families and will do well together. I never cared overly much for a marriage to be based on love. You know I've always been practical with those types of things."

Olivia nodded, looking out over the gardens, bewildered at her friend's words. If she did not love Lord Oglemoore, then why could she not leave him be? Leave him for her?

The sound of a carriage approaching caught her attention, and Olivia glanced to where the road leading into the estate became visible through the trees. A black, highly polished carriage flittered through the foliage—more guests she assumed.

Athol shot to her feet, checking her gown and hair. "This will be Lord Oglemoore now. He said he'd arrive today. I'm so thankful that Lady Clara was willing to invite him and his friend to stay for the house party too."

Olivia did not move, not sure if her legs would support her. What a fun party they would all make with the man she had pinned all her hopes upon and her best friend who was trying as hard as she might to gain an understanding with him. She inwardly groaned, wanting to vanish to her rooms instead of meeting the guests as she should.

"Come, Olivia. Let us go out to the front and welcome them."

Olivia nodded, following without a word. Athol strode ahead, every now and then stopping to call for Olivia to quicken her pace. They made the estate front just as the carriage rocked to a halt, a billow of dust and all.

Her cousin Lady Clara and her husband, Mr. Grant, were already waiting on the home's steps, a warm smile on their lips as they prepared to greet their guests. Clara met Olivia's gaze. Puzzlement crossed her features before she joined her on the graveled drive.

"Are you well, Olivia dear? You look somewhat pale." She reached out, touching her forehead. "You do not feel warm, is there something else that is bothering you?"

Besides the fact that her best friend wanted to marry the man she coveted as her husband, no everything was perfectly well. "It is nothing, I assure you. Perhaps I have had too much sun today."

A footman opened the carriage door, and Lord Oglemoore jumped out, clasping Mr. Grant's—Stephen to those who knew him well—hands in welcome. He then turned to Athol, who stood waiting close by. Pleasure crossed his features, and Olivia felt the devastation of his attachment to her friend to her core. He liked her, to his credit. More than she'd thought, considering Athol merely liked the fellow, not actually loved him. Even so, Lord Oglemoore smiled lovingly at her friend, and Olivia did not miss the blush that stole across her friend's cheeks.

The carriage dipped a second time, and another gentleman appeared in the door. Olivia glanced at the man who jumped out of the equipage, dismissing him when Lord Oglemoore spoke.

"How wonderful to be back here again. It has been too long, Lady Clara, since you've opened the house," he said, smiling at her cousin before his gaze met hers.

He stepped toward her but did not drop Athol's hand that sat upon his arm. "Miss Quinton. You are a welcome sight, to be sure. I hope you're well?"

Somehow in all the despondency that pumped through her veins, she remembered her manners and smiled. "I am well, Lord Oglemoore. It is good to see you again too."

Oglemoore gestured to the gentleman behind him, and for the first time, Olivia took in the other house guest. He was taller than his lordship, athletic in build and surprisingly handsome.

She frowned, feeling as if she'd met him before, but unable to place where.

He smiled in welcome, a contemplative look in his eye when his gaze landed on her.

"This is my friend, His Grace, the Duke of Hamlyn."

Stephen held out his hand to His Grace, shaking it. "It has been too long, Hamlyn. I'm glad you're able to make the trip to Kent."

"Thank you for having me stay and congratulations on your marriage," the duke said, in a honeyed, deep tone.

Olivia watched as the duke kissed her cousin's cheeks. She turned for the doors, ready to go inside where she may be able to slip away for a moment or two to gather her wits. The house party loomed like a week of torture, and she wasn't so sure she wanted to be here anymore.

Her escape was blocked when Clara caught up to her,

leading her into the drawing room where an array of refreshments and a light lunch were prepared.

"Where do you think you're disappearing to, my dear? You have guests whom you must help me with."

Olivia sighed, letting Clara lead her into the room. "I need to speak to you when you are free. It is imperative."

Clara glanced at her, her brow furrowed. "Of course. I knew something was troubling you. We shall speak as soon as we can."

"Thank you." Olivia blinked away the sting of tears as she watched Athol and Lord Oglemoore seat themselves together on the settee by the window that overlooked the river. The duke hovered near the unlit hearth, speaking to Stephen.

"I'll come to your room before dinner this evening, and we'll have a chat," Clara said, patting her hand in comfort.

"Thank you." Olivia seated herself on a single leather-backed chair, willing the time to go by fast. A shadow passed over her and she glanced up, only to meet the amused gaze of the duke. She raised one brow, contesting his inspection of her with one of her own. "Is something amiss, Your Grace? You're scrutinizing me as if I have a blemish on my nose." Her question was, she supposed, rather rude, but she was no longer in the mood to be congenial. When one's hope of happiness was stripped, one was allowed to be curt.

"I do believe we've met, Miss Quinton. Last Season, in fact," he answered, his lips catching Olivia's attention for a moment before she tore her gaze away.

She shrugged, not willing to admit she knew him as well. A passing acquaintance and nothing more. He certainly never asked her to dance, she remembered that all too well. "It is possible that our paths crossed, Your Grace. I've met many people over the last few years in London." Pity he had not deemed her worthy of his interest, for he was known as a most sought-after catch.

He kneeled beside her chair, his hand resting on the arm. Olivia glanced at it. Really, did the man have to invade her space as well as ask her questions about a Season she'd prefer to forget?

"I assumed when you did not return to London this year that you had married." A light blush stole across his cheeks. Olivia narrowed her eyes, undecided if she would let him get away with what he was implying, that she was still unwed, an old maid in the making.

"I did not think gentlemen cared whether women they hardly favored to know married or not." He glanced at her, an amused look she found annoying filling his eyes. Did the man have no shame?

"I merely was surprised that an intelligent and beautiful woman such as yourself had not been swooped off her feet and carried into the sunset. That is all."

Olivia shut her mouth with a snap and tore her gaze away from him. He did not need to be so forward as that. Nor did she like his light flirtation with her. She did not want it from the duke.

She wanted it from Lord Oglemoore. Not that that was a possibility since the gentleman had his whole purpose fixed on her best friend. "I have not found anything to tempt me to the altar, my lord."

"Is that so?" he stated, glancing at his friend and then back to her. Olivia refused to blush or break her gaze. To do so would give credence to what he was saying, and she would not give him that pleasure. He continued to stare, not giving an inch on their little challenge and her blush deepened, their fixation on each other growing awkward.

Stephen cleared his throat, coming to stand beside Olivia.

"Everything well, my dear?" he asked her, touching her shoulder.

Olivia nodded, cursing that she had to look away before others noticed their frivolous game and made a comment.

"Of course. His Grace was just telling me how fond he is of your home and would like a tour," she lied.

Olivia stood and strode from the room before her cousin's husband asked if she would do the honors. Under no circumstance was she in the mood to play tour guide, and certainly not to a man who seemed amused by what was going on between her and Lord Oglemoore.

She strode toward the stairs, not caring she did not resemble the duke's granddaughter she was. She needed to reach the sanctity of her room. A place she could think and plan.

What that plan was, however, she was not certain just yet. Would she try to dissuade Athol into marrying Lord Oglemoore should he ask? Over the years, she'd certainly heard plenty of tales about the gentleman's antics both in London and Bath.

Some of which had made even herself blush a time or two, but after his kindness toward her last Season she had dismissed the stories as false.

Olivia made her room, closing and locking the door before she flopped onto the bed. How could this have happened? She had been so sure of his regard for her. Last Season, Lord Oglemoore sought her out, danced and took supper with her. The horrible thought crossed her mind that it was all for show, a game he enjoyed to play with unattached women.

She sighed, staring up at the wooden beams lining her bedroom ceiling. There were two choices she could make regarding this awful turn of events. She could wish them well and move on with her life. Have another Season and see if any offers were forthcoming.

To parade herself again would be a humiliation she doubted she could ever recover from, and she wasn't certain she had it in her to do again. To walk into a ballroom, night after night, and try to find love.

She swiped a tear from her cheek, annoyance thrumming through her. Athol deserved better than a man who would treat her friend or any woman with so little respect. What was stopping him from throwing Athol aside when someone better in his opinion came along? Nothing.

Olivia sat up, thinking of what could be done. He would pay for his callousness. She would show Athol he was unworthy of her during the week that he was here. Olivia chewed her bottom lip, frowning in thought. But how, that was the question, and one she would mull over before tomorrow.

CHAPTER 2

*L*ater that evening, Jasper sat before the hearth in the blue salon, sipping a whisky and thinking over Miss Olivia Quinton. He could not fathom why his friend Oglemoore had not courted the woman himself. She was a beautiful lady. In fact, he'd almost choked on his own tongue when they had been introduced for a second time. She had changed from the last time they had met. Her body had transformed into a generous feminine curve. Breasts that a man's hands hungered to knead. Hips one wanted to press against one's own. She would look absolutely stunning lying pliant and ready, wet and willing before him.

He adjusted his seat as footsteps sounded on the wooden passage leading to the salon.

"Ah, Hamlyn, just the man I wished to see. May I join you in a drink?" Oglemoore asked, striding into the room toward the decanter of whisky.

"Of course." Jasper observed the flames in the hearth as they licked at the wood, conflicted over his agreement with his friend to seduce Miss Quinton so as to make his life more palatable. If Oglemoore had shown more affection than he ought, then he needed to face the consequences of his actions and man up.

"What a day we've had. Thank you again for distracting Miss Quinton after dinner. I know she harbors feelings for me, but I'm hoping when she sees me with her friend, and you show a keen interest, her own emotional connection will wane."

Jasper sighed, rubbing the back of his neck, doubting Miss Quinton would do any such thing. She might be quite displeased to have been treated as a fool in London by Oglemoore. "She did not appear enthralled by my attempt to speak with her. It did not help that because I had not danced with her in London, I was seen as wanting. I cannot see how this plan of yours will work, Oglemoore. Miss Quinton has thorns, and they're aimed at my ass."

"I'm asking that you distract her from me. Marriage is not a requirement. You simply need to show her there are other options for her. She needs to see that whatever misapprehension she was living under regarding myself was misplaced."

Jasper narrowed his eyes, not understanding how his friend could not see that his interest in the chit could lead to the same problem Oglemoore now had with her.

"I do not understand you, Oglemoore. Why not marry Miss Quinton instead of Lady Athol? I confess," Jasper said, leaning back in his chair and folding one leg over the other. "She was not as I remembered her. Miss Quinton is far superior in appearances than I recalled."

"Hmm," Oglemoore said, frowning into his glass of whisky. "Which is exactly why she would not suit me. I'm a jealous sod. I dislike my paramours being ogled, nevertheless my wife. Miss Quinton is beautiful, I grant you, but Athol is more to my taste. She is rich, but not too handsome that she will be plucked from my arms by some fiend. You've seen how invidious I become when anyone compliments my paramour."

"You are not going to part ways with Heidi, then?" The idea repulsed Jasper. If a gentleman were going to marry, he ought to respect his wife enough to separate from his mistress. His parents had a loveless marriage, and he would not wish that on any wife or child.

Oglemoore's jaw clenched at his words. "Whoever ends up as my wife will not know that I have a mistress. Heidi is of no consequence to this discussion."

"I wish you well with that," Jasper said, knowing full well he wasn't ready for a wife or to lose his own mistress Lotty, and wouldn't ask anyone to be his wife until he was ready to. It had taken him some weeks to wear his mistress down, gain her trust. He didn't particularly want to lose the arrangement they had simply because his friend had tangled himself into a bind and needed saving. If Miss Quinton thought him in earnest to gain her affections, his life as a bachelor in London would be over.

"How am I to distract her from you when she does not want anything to do with me? Did you see her today? She all but bolted from the room at the mere mention of giving me a tour. If that does not show a woman determined not to be pursued by me, I'll eat my own gloves."

"Display some of that English charm I hear you possess. Miss Quinton will not be able to deny you her friendship. You merely have to distract her, not sleep with her."

Jasper sighed, a noose settling about his neck, threatening to choke him. This would not end well. Women, in general, always saw a man's attention for more than it may be. It gave them hope where there was not always hope to have. He liked Miss Quinton, and to play her a fool for a second time was not right. Nor could he allow his friend to marry a woman he did not want. That, too, would be unfair for Miss Quinton.

"I shall continue my friendship with her, but I shall not be seducing her or taking any privileges she may offer if she starts to believe she and I have a future together. I do not want to become embroiled in a scandal that sees my leg shackled to her. If I do, you can be guaranteed I shall not be the only one going down with the ship, Oglemoore. I shall be pulling you down under with me," he said, his tone severe.

Oglemoore glanced at him, all seriousness and joking wiped from his visage. "Thank you for your assistance, Hamlyn. Know that I do not want to hurt Miss Quinton any more than you do. I'm happy for you to be friends and nothing more so long as she stops wishing that she'll turn my head, and I'll offer to her instead."

Jasper raised his brow, wanting that to be true, and yet his unease would not dissipate. This could end badly for all of them.

*O*livia snuck away the next afternoon after lunch to her favorite location in the garden. An old oak sat before the river's edge, not far from her cousin's home, where she'd spent many hours lying on the grassy bank, reading, drawing, dreaming of a future whenever she visited here.

Her future after the last Season she'd hoped would include Lord Oglemoore, but that was not to be. He was not interested in her as he once had been, which in itself ought to vex her. The idea he'd used her poorly, teased her with the idea of them, hurt.

She caught sight of the man himself, walking with Athol and the duke. Together, His Grace was a striking man against

Lord Oglemoore. Taller, broader across the shoulders, long, lean legs that looked well-toned from years of horse-riding. He was a handsome gentleman. No doubt turned the heads of many fine ladies. His buckskin breeches and black jacket fitted him to perfection, and he looked comfortable and at ease within himself. Sure of his own capabilities and situation.

She narrowed her eyes, thinking of a way to repay Lord Oglemoore's treatment. Of how she could show him what he'd overlooked by choosing another, even if that person was her best friend and someone she would not allow him to misuse either.

Olivia turned away, leaning upon the tree and watching the river's water idly float by. Her plan was not without merit, but she needed a gentleman willing to help her tease Lord Oglemoore into thinking he'd made a mistake.

"Good afternoon, Miss Quinton. What a lovely situation in which you have found yourself."

Olivia gasped, looking up to find His Grace staring down at her, a silly, lopsided smile on his lips. The scent of sandalwood and pine teased her senses. Heavens, he smelled nice for a man, as if he'd bathed in the forest just for her.

The thought of His Grace naked and lathing his skin in hot, scented water sent a frisson of longing through her. Her cheeks warmed.

"As you see," she said, turning to pick up her sketch pad and slapping it onto her lap. "Can I help you with anything, Your Grace?"

He sat beside her, leaning back on his elbows, continuing to admire the river. "I saw you just now, peeping from behind the oak." He gestured to her paper. "What are you drawing, may I ask?"

"Nothing of importance," she replied, closing her sketch pad. "Was there anything else that you wanted? Or do you simply intend to while away the afternoon in my presence?"

Not that she minded his company, but now that she'd thought of her idea on how to make Lord Oglemoore pay, she needed time to think about her plan. The duke, as handsome and nice as it was for him to be sitting beside her, made her mind less clear. She was unable to concentrate as much as she should.

Laughter lurked in his blue orbs, and he grinned. "Would that be so very bad if I wished to do exactly that?" he asked, meeting her gaze.

He truly did have lovely eyes. A darker, stormier shade of blue than Lord Oglemoore's. "Is there nothing more stimulating you could be doing than lying here with me? I do not have a chaperone. It's not seemly for you to be here."

His Grace glanced over his shoulder and then turned back to her, shrugging. The wickedness of his features told Olivia all she needed to know about this man. He was a consummate rake and well used to getting his own way.

"I can be seen from the house, and since I do not have you in my arms while I ravish that pretty, delectable mouth of yours, there will be no harm done."

Olivia stared at him, unable to believe he had said something so shocking. Ravish her pretty, delectable mouth? The idea of him kissing her, of pulling her hard against his chest... It would be wicked and thrilling to experience. And if Lord Oglemoore happened to see them...

"You cannot say such things to me, Your Grace." Yet, the thought he may stop at her chastisement was equally annoying. She was not so proud as to admit that while in London, she had enjoyed the attentions of Lord Oglemoore. That his consideration now seemed to be elsewhere was another point altogether. Having the duke admit he found her enticing was, in itself, a nice boost to her soul and helpful to her plan.

Olivia studied the man at her side a moment, his teasing

grin firmly set on his delectable lips. If he were so bold to her, nothing was stopping her from doing the same. She was, after all, a duke's granddaughter. High enough on the peerage ladder that His Grace would not dare to slight her publicly at her words. "Your Grace, since you're quite willing to speak plainly, may I do also?"

He raised his brows, a curious light in his eyes. "Please, say whatever comes to mind, Miss Quinton."

"You may call me Olivia if you prefer."

Pleasure stole across his features before he said, "I would like that very much, Olivia. You, in turn, may call me Jasper or Hamlyn if that is more comfortable."

Jasper? The name suited him. It was nice to hear a name that was different from the norm. Not another boring Arthur or William. "I would like to have your assistance with a concern I'm having, but it is one that is quite personal and sensitive, if I'm honest."

He leaned his head on one hand, watching her keenly. At some point, he'd picked up a piece of straw and slipped it between his lips. The sight of his tongue flicking the tiny plant from side to side made her stomach flutter. The man was awfully distracting.

"Intriguing, Olivia. Do tell," he teased her, wickedness dancing in his eyes.

Olivia took a deep, fortifying breath to say what she must. This was for the best. Oglemoore must pay for his crime. "I need your assistance, Jasper. I need you to help me portray that we're courting, and possibly falling in love. I need you to do this with me to prove Lord Oglemoore for the fiend he is. I know, he is your friend, and I'm sorry for speaking ill of him, but he played me the fool last year and he shall not get away with it, or court my friend only to throw her aside as well. Will you help me with this?"

There, she had done it. Said the words she'd not thought

to ever utter to a man, and not just any man, but one she hardly knew. But what better ally to help her with her revenge than his best friend? If one was to become jealous over affections, one must be in the mind's eye at all times. The duke was always about Lord Oglemoore. It was the perfect plan.

His tongue halted flicking the straw. He pulled it out, throwing it aside. "Let me understand this. You wish for me to court you to make Oglemoore jealous and therefore want you back, only this time you will tell him to go hang and in turn prove to your friend Lady Athol that she is better rid of his lordship and his fickle nature?"

She nodded. "Yes, that is exactly what I propose. Are you a willing participant, or do I need to find someone else?"

CHAPTER 3

*B*loody hell. He could not believe what Miss Quinton proposed. Had she really asked for him to help her torment Oglemoore? His friend had asked him to befriend her only two days ago, distract her from his courtship with Athol. Were the two of them playing some sort of game on him he wasn't aware of? What were the odds of both of them asking for such assistance?

What had he managed to get himself into now?

Her eagerness, her desire to right the wrong Oglemoore had bestowed upon her pulled at a place within him he'd not thought he had. He reached out, sliding a finger across her jaw, taking in the few freckles that sat across the bridge of her nose. Hell, she was pretty, sweet, and headstrong, a woman to be reckoned with and one who had asked for his assistance. He could not deny her, nor could he stop assisting Oglemoore. He would do as both asked and hoped he survived the ordeal.

One boon of helping Miss Quinton was that he could be near her person whenever he wished. After all, she was handsome, and someone had he taken the time to meet last Season, may have flirted with the idea of courting himself.

"What would it entail should I assist you?" he asked, sliding his thumb across her bottom lip. "Can I touch you as I am now?" Her lips were smooth and as soft as a feather. His body hardened at the idea of teasing his friend Oglemoore into imagining he'd made an error for his choice of bride. Of the stolen kisses Miss Quinton may now allow.

This house party may not be such a bore after all...

"Well, we can stroll about the house and gardens together. Always look as if we have important things to discuss, have our heads together, that sort of thing. Hand-holding, but only when Lord Oglemoore is about so he may catch us. You must stare at me adoringly and often."

He stared at her now, adoringly, and knew all too well it would not be an effort to pretend to like this woman. Not that he wanted to marry her or anyone, but to pretend, well, that was safe, was it not? They were deceiving everyone else, not themselves. It was the perfect way in which to satisfy both his promise to Oglemoore and Miss Quinton.

"Is that all I'm allowed? What about a stolen kiss or two? How I touched you just now? If we know Oglemoore will see it, what harm could that do, do you think?"

A pretty blush kissed her cheeks. He grinned, lying back on his arms to stare up at the sky through the dappled leaves of the oak above them. "I must admit that to kiss you would be no chore, Olivia."

He heard her small intake of breath. "We cannot kiss, Your Grace. That would be too scandalous," she said, her tone outraged, along with her features.

He chuckled. "Pity," he sighed. "I could teach you so you would be an expert by the time the gentlemen of the *ton* do come to their senses and offer for your hand. A man such as the marquess would know how to kiss a woman, and you should be prepared if you wish to marry."

"You think I'm terribly wicked for doing this to Oglemoore, do you not?" she asked, a frown between her perfect brows. "My friend must come to her senses and see him for the fiend he is. I will not let him get her hopes up only to disappoint her as he has done to me."

He glanced at her and reached out to smooth the small line away. "If you believe this is truly a mistake and your friend is yet to find the man whom she will love with all her heart, then perhaps not so bad. But," he said, his hand dropping to his side, "should Oglemoore turn out to be a good match for your friend, and you hurt Athol through this scheme, then you risk losing more than you would gain."

She sighed, lifting up her knees to lean atop them. "No matter what I do, this I promise you, Your Grace. I shall not throw myself at your friend, no matter how he reacts to our flirting. I shall allow Athol to see that his affections are not honorable toward her and that she should not marry him. As for Athol's own affections, I believe they are not engaged. Not as one's emotions should be, I assume. I think, therefore, what I am doing is a service, not an injustice."

The sound of laughter caught their attention, and they both watched as Oglemoore and Athol strode together, arms linked, into the house.

Jasper took the opportunity to study Olivia. How was it that a woman such as herself had not been swooped up and carried down to the altar already? Was she so set upon Oglemoore that she'd failed to see who else was trying to gain her attention?

"We're quite hidden here under this oak, and even though you can be seen from the house in this position, I do not think that is the case. Perhaps you ought to lean down and kiss me now, Olivia. We can start your kissing lessons early."

She gasped, staring at him, but the small, teasing light in her eyes told him she was intrigued. He sat up, placing his face as close to hers as he dared. "Have you ever kissed a man before?" he whispered, his attention dipping to her sweet, sensual lips.

"No," she murmured. The reply pleased him. He didn't want to think of her kissing anyone else, and certainly not Oglemoore. He did not know where that odd thought came from, and he pushed it aside for later evaluation.

"All you have to do is lean a fraction closer and touch your lips to mine." He reached out and caressed her hand, relishing the feel of her soft skin. "Kiss me, Olivia." Her gaze dipped to his lips, and he leaned closer still. So near now that he could almost taste her. "Use me to make Oglemoore pay for his crime." If this is what both Olivia and Oglemoore wanted, Jasper would serve them both well. He may not have always wanted the position he was placed in, but this turn of events was fortunate indeed.

He would enjoy everything she would give and be a good friend to both her and Oglemoore at the same time. It was indeed a perfect plan.

*A*t the mention of the marquess, Olivia's decision to kiss the duke was made. She closed the small gap between them and pressed her mouth to his. For a moment, she did not move, simply kept her mouth shut and against his, feeling for the first time what a man's lips felt like. His were warm and so very soft. She had not expected that from him. Her mind whirled at the idea of kissing him whenever she liked, and she found herself quite excited about teasing Oglemoore over the next week with her new beau.

If she hoped for a ravishing kiss, she was utterly wrong. Hamlyn did none of those things. Oh no, he did something so much worse. His hands cradled her face, tipping her head to one side as his mouth explored hers in languorous, deep strokes that made her toes curl in her silk slippers.

He tasted of tea and strawberries. The kiss was unlike anything she'd ever experienced before. It was raw, new, and addicting. How many women had this rogue kissed to know how to make a woman purr?

Olivia pushed the unhelpful thought aside, not wanting to think about how many women he may have had in his life. Men, such as the duke, kissed many women. She wasn't a simpleton to believe she was his first.

But maybe you could be his last...

Heat pooled between her legs, a reaction that was new and wonderful. The idea of crawling onto his lap, of rubbing herself up against him to soothe the ache that thrummed at her core taunted her. This kiss stole her wits. Made her want things no well-bred young woman ought to want.

This kiss was dangerous. How unexpected and pleasant.

Olivia pulled back, staring at him, trying to right her addled mind. Any kiss she shared with the duke—Jasper, as he wanted her to call him—was not supposed to muddle her mind and distract her from her plan.

His Grace had one purpose and one purpose only. To make Oglemoore jealous, to make him show his true colors and nothing more.

Her mind whirled with thoughts, anything to diminish the fact she may have just experienced a kiss she would dream about for years to come. Long to do over again and again.

His Grace studied her, a curious look in his eyes.

"Do you think Oglemoore saw our kiss?" she said, tearing her gaze away from Hamlyn and looking back at the house where they'd seen Oglemoore and Athol last. Anywhere but the handsome face that tempted her more than it ought. More than Oglemoore ever had.

Oglemoore was nowhere to be seen, and a small part of her was thankful for it.

"I do not believe so."

Olivia glanced at Hamlyn, not missing his curt, annoyed tone. With a small shake of his head, he stood, brushing down his breeches. "Shall we return indoors, Miss Quinton?"

Unsure what his lordship's matter was, she shook her head, leaning back against the tree. "No, I shall remain here a while longer. Thank you again for your assistance, Your Grace. I look forward to seeing you at dinner this evening," she said, not giving voice to her concern toward his suddenly cool demeanor.

"Of course, good afternoon." He strode from her, back straight and hands fisted at his sides. She narrowed her eyes. Perhaps he had not liked kissing her as much as she enjoyed kissing him. He'd kissed many women, and this was a game after all.

Olivia picked up her sketch pad and pencil and started to draw the river, supposing it may all be in her imagination that he was rather put out. She would be a fool indeed if she thought his kisses meant anything more than their agreement.

She made a terrible error of judgment with Oglemoore. She would not make the same mistake with the duke.

CHAPTER 4

"I saw you this afternoon sitting with Duke Hamlyn. Do tell me if he's showing an interest in you, Olivia. If you become attached to his grace, perhaps we can have a double wedding," Athol said, grinning across the bed from Olivia as they drank hot chocolate before retiring for the night.

Athol had stolen into her room after she had procured two cups of hot chocolate, and now it would seem that at least Athol had noticed her outing with the duke. Did that mean Lord Oglemoore had too?

"I was sketching the river, and he joined me, nothing more. Please do not read into his attentions any further than that."

"I will not. I promise," Athol said, finishing her cup of chocolate and placing it on the bedside cabinet. "I wanted to talk with you about something, and I want you to be honest with me."

"Of course," Olivia said without thought, wondering what it was Athol had to say. Perhaps Lord Oglemoore had asked her to be his wife already, and her plans on making him pay were lost already. The thought soured her hot chocolate on her tongue.

"Elliott mentioned he thought that you may have been upset with him upon his arrival. Say it isn't so. I need you both to be friends, to like each other if I'm to marry him."

Olivia choked on her drink and coughed. Did Lord Oglemoore suspect her past hopes toward him? Oh, how mortifying!

"What makes you think such a thing?" she asked, frowning, and in truth, not wishing to know how Athol, or Elliott —since her friend seemed to be on a first-name basis with Lord Oglemoore—would think such a thing. Only Hamlyn knew of her plan, and he would not dare tell anyone.

"I was having afternoon tea with Elliott today, and he mentioned it in conversation. I know he grew quite fond of you when you were in town last year, but I'm sure he was just being polite. It would not make sense that he is courting me now if he wanted you as his bride last Season." Athol giggled, but Olivia could hear the nervousness in her friend's tone. "Do you not agree?"

Athol was not the type of friend to believe words Olivia would state about Oglemoore, she needed to see with her own eyes what type of man he was. If she could make the marquess show what his true make up was, she was certain Athol would not marry him.

"Lord Oglemoore was one of the kindest, most honest gentlemen I met last year in town. I would hope he would not play any woman a fool. If he has asked you to be his bride, I'm certain that our friendship was nothing more than that…a benign friendship." Not that Olivia believed that for a moment. The fiend had used her, played her like a string on a harp, and had now seemingly moved on to greener pastures. Well, she would not allow it. He would pay, or she'd die trying to make it so.

Athol frowned, staring down at her clasped hands in her lap. "He has not asked me yet, but I expect him to any day. I am, after all, an heiress and an earl's daughter. Surely it is only a matter of days before he offers me his hand."

Olivia stared at her friend, unsure she'd ever heard her sound so desperate to have a husband. What had come over her? "Lord Oglemoore and I did spend time together in town, but I'm sure you do not have anything to worry about. It seems he has chosen you to be his wife, even if he has not yet voiced such declarations out loud." Olivia could not help but plant the seed of doubt in her friend's mind. She no longer trusted Oglemoore to be true, and Athol deserved much better than him. Marriage, after all, was a lifelong commitment. One did not want to make a mistake.

At her friend's worried frown, a pang of guilt pinched her conscience. She did not want them to be at odds over a gentleman, but Oglemoore had been overly familiar with her. What else was she to think but that he wanted to court her? Possibly marry her. His being here at her cousin's house party, she had thought, was proof of his attachment. The Quinton pride ran deep, and it wasn't in Olivia to simply leave things as they were and move on. She had thought her hunt for a husband over. She could not simply walk away and allow his lordship to get away with what he had done, nor could she allow Athol to marry such a man. A flippant, untrustworthy one.

Athol had said herself she had multiple gentlemen seeking her hand. Why did she want Oglemoore anyway? She did not love him.

"He will voice them soon, I feel. I think you shall find before the house party comes to an end, I shall be happily betrothed to Lord Oglemoore."

Olivia smiled at her friend's words, not wishing to say any more on the matter. "What do you think of Duke

Hamlyn?" she asked, the reminder of his kiss this afternoon still fresh in her mind. Of how her body had turned to liquid heat. He was simply the perfect vessel to make another man rue the day.

"He's so very handsome, Olivia. When Elliott introduced me for the first time, I imagined myself rather in love with him and somewhat mad at myself that I had allowed Oglemoore to believe I was in love with him more."

"He does have a pleasing face," Olivia conceded, not wanting to give too much away. It was not like their repartee was true and possibly the start of something between them.

"Pleasing face," Athol mocked. "I wager it's more than pleasing. Hamlyn's face is sculpted to precision. His eyes are the deepest shade of blue I've ever seen. As for his aristocratic, perfect nose and lips that were made for sin, I wager he's more than pleasing. That he's here in Kent and for a whole week, la, I'll wager the ladies in London are most displeased."

"That does not mean anything," Olivia said, watching the flames in the hearth. She already knew what those lips felt like, how they incited a need she'd not known she possessed. He was too handsome for his own good and had a sweet temperament that was equally charming. Not many gentlemen would help her taunt a fellow friend into believing they had chosen the wrong woman to marry.

"It means a great deal," Athol argued. "It means you may have a chance of winning him. He certainly looks at you a great deal. Why at dinner this evening, I often caught him watching you, listening to your every word. He appeared very much in awe of you, in fact."

Warmth filtered through her at the thought of the duke being interested in her outside her own scheme. Surely not. He was one of London's rogues. On top of that, she was sure she'd heard he had a longtime mistress set up in town.

"What did he look at me like?" she asked anyway, despite her own warnings to herself and the fact it didn't matter how he observed her. It was all a game anyway and not real life.

"We're both maids," Athol continued. "But the duke watched you this evening as a rake watches his prey. Contemplated all the naughty things you could do together if you were alone."

"Athol!" Olivia gaped, as her friend laughed and shrugged.

"It's true, no matter what you may say to the contrary. The next time you're around Hamlyn, I suggest you watch him, catch him yourself eyeing you, and then you will see what I say is true."

Olivia could not believe it was so, but what if it were? The duke certainly seemed put out this afternoon with her. Was he jealous? It was not possible! They had an agreement. She was seeing things where there was nothing to be seen at all. Even if the idea of the duke's interest in her was enticing and flattering notion to consider.

"I shall observe His Grace and get back to you on my findings. We shall discuss the matter at the end of the house party."

Athol slid off the bed, a mischievous grin on her lips. "A wager? Five pounds says he becomes an admirer of yours."

Olivia held out her hand, shaking her friend's. "That is a wager I'm willing to take." And win, considering the duke's attention on her this evening like a besotted fool was merely part of his acting as if enamored of her already. Poor Athol, she did not stand a chance at winning this bet. The five pounds was hers for the taking.

$\mathcal{J}$asper thundered across the land at blistering speed, his mount well worth the thousand pounds he paid for the gelding he'd had sent for from London for the duration of the house party. The horse was fast, strong, and capable, and went a long way in distracting him from the alluring Miss Quinton back at Chidding Hall.

Oglemoore, he could see out the corner of his eye, could not keep up to his mount's speed. He laughed aloud, knowing how much that fact would annoy his friend. Jasper pulled on the reins, slowing to a walk.

"Ah, this is living, do you not agree?" Oglemoore said, pulling his mount up alongside Jasper.

He nodded, relishing the green, picturesque fields of the late Duke of Law's lands. "It is beautiful here. I can see why Lady Clara invited us all down to Kent for a well needed distraction during the Season."

"Yes, and speaking of distraction, how is your courting of Miss Quinton coming along? I can assume by the fact she's not been chasing me about the estate that it is going better than I planned."

Jasper thought about how he would reply. He was, in fact, working for both parties, but for different reasons. His friend Oglemoore to keep Miss Quinton from having designs on him, and Miss Quinton to make Oglemoore regret his choice of bride and to stop him from gaining her friend Athol. A muddle anyone could make an error performing.

Jasper hoped for both his friend's and Miss Quinton's sake he could be of assistance, but he was starting to doubt that he would. After his kiss with Olivia yesterday, his mind had been less clear on his conduct and the rules he'd promised to obey.

His own rules regarding his life and his decision not to yet look for a wife himself.

She was a handsome woman, intelligent, if not a little misguided by her past affection for a man who clearly sought his future elsewhere. "We are becoming better acquainted," he answered, not wanting to tell Oglemoore everything that had passed between them. "I shall keep her occupied enough that she will not trouble you while we're here."

Oglemoore grinned. "I knew I could count on you. There are few women who would not look for a diversion in your arms, a verified rake that you are. But keep in mind, I do not wish for you to seduce her. That would be unfair to Miss Quinton."

The whole of Oglemoore's plan seemed unfair to Jasper already, but with Miss Quinton having her own scheme, he could not see the harm in assisting them both. So long as neither found out.

"Tell me," he said, changing the subject, "what is new between you and Lady Athol? Are you certain you want to marry the chit now that you're spending more time with her?"

Oglemoore looked out over the land, a frown between his brow. "I believe so. She's a sensible woman and compliments me well. I kissed her the other evening and was quite pleased with the outcome."

Jasper stared at his friend. *Pleased with the outcome?* Whatever sort of reaction to a kiss was that? After he'd kissed Olivia, he'd all but lost his wits. He'd forgotten entirely his scheme with his friend and the one the lady herself had made him promise to follow. All he'd thought of afterward were her soft lips. Her sweet exhale when he'd deepened the embrace. He wanted to do it again with a need that was foreign to him. The idea of kissing Miss Quinton outdid his desire to see his mistress in town. And he received far more than kisses from his mistress. An odd reaction, no doubt.

"Was the kiss not as passionate as you would like?" Jasper asked, adjusting his grip on the reins.

Oglemoore shrugged. "It was pleasing, but," he sighed, running a hand through his hair, "Lady Athol is a hard nut to crack. I do not think she allows her emotions to come to the fore. I had hoped she would be more passionate when I kissed her for the first time, but she was not. I'm unsure of how to make her respond to me."

"Do you think her feelings are engaged?" Jasper certainly knew from Miss Quinton that she believed they were not. The thought that Olivia's scheme in making his friend regret his choice left a cold shiver to run down his spine. He didn't want her to be anyone's second choice, not even his friend's. Oglemoore no longer deserved her attachment. He'd chosen another, and he ought to live with that decision.

Miss Quinton deserved to be loved for the strong, amusing, competent woman she was. Not simply because his friend could not engage another woman's desire and make her fall at his feet as he would like.

"I shall continue to court her and hope for the best." Oglemoore waggled his brows, mischief in his gaze. "I can always fall back to Miss Quinton, I suppose. She will always be there waiting in the wings should Lady Athol turn out to be a cold fish."

Jasper schooled his features, disdain for his friend running hot through his veins. There was no way in hell he'd allow Miss Quinton back into Oglemoore's arms after how he just spoke. As for Lady Athol, Olivia was right, she too deserved better than Oglemoore. What was wrong with the man that he spoke in such a demeaning, unlikeable way toward women?

Marriage may not be a situation he wished to be involved in at present, but he did hope that when he decided to marry, he would desire his bride, want her in his bed, and beside him in all things. Oglemoore spoke of marriage with such aloofness that it turned his stomach.

They fell into an uncomfortable silence, at least on Jasper's part. Oglemoore did not seem to have noticed that his words were offensive. "Enough with all the talk of the ladies present, shall we go for a run? Stretch our horse's legs?" Oglemoore said, kicking his mount into a gallop and sprinting ahead.

Jasper let him gain some distance, content to canter behind and mull over his friendship with Oglemoore and his developing one with Miss Quinton. He liked her, and one truth he did know was she was not for his friend, and he'd ensure that at the end of the house party, that remained the case.

CHAPTER 6

There was something seriously wrong with her. Olivia sat in the blue drawing room upstairs and watched as Lord Oglemoore and the duke played a game of piquet. For all her distress at having to watch Oglemoore court her friend, it was not his lordship who held her attention this day.

With a will of their own, her eyes kept flicking up from the book she read to Hamlyn. A small lock of hair kept falling over his brow, and he seemed to frown and bite his lip when he concentrated on his game.

She bit back a smile. He was simply the most adorable piquet player she'd ever beheld and from looking at his distress, not the best one either.

Her cousin Clara sat beside her on the settee, meeting Olivia's amused grin with one of her own. "Your attention is marked toward a certain gentleman guest. Is there something you would like to tell your favorite cousin?"

Olivia placed her book in her lap, shushing her friend and family member. "Of course not. You should not say such things, and out loud, mind you. Someone may hear."

"Hmm," Clara said, glancing at the table where the men sat. "You have a particular look that I always see on a fox before it lunges at a rabbit. Contemplation, deliberation, what the rabbit may taste like."

Olivia gasped, shushing her cousin. "Clara! You need to behave." She chuckled despite herself. "In any case, I did not know you've been hunting lately and knew how foxes look at rabbits."

Clara grinned. "Let me just admit to knowing the look well. I am married, after all." She paused, settling farther on the settee and moving nearer to Olivia. "Hamlyn is very handsome. He seems to only get better with age. Like a good red wine, I would say."

"Remember, you're married, my dear."

Clara glanced at her husband, who sat opposite them, reading a book. Her cousin's features softened, and love all but glowed from her eyes. "I'm not looking at anyone else, I promise you. But I am a woman, and I do see your regard. I thought your heart was set on Oglemoore. That was certainly what town gossip had to say."

Olivia swallowed the awful thought that she was being gossiped about in town and in part annoyed that society had picked up on their friendship that blossomed last year. It only proved yet again he had shown considerable attention toward her and ought to be ashamed of himself being here and courting her friend.

She glanced at Oglemoore and caught him watching her. She turned back to Clara, unsure what that look meant, and no longer caring what it did mean. "At this point in time, I doubt I shall ever marry. I will admit that Hamlyn has been friendly and affable toward me. We get along quite well." So well, in fact, that his kiss still made the blood in her veins pump fast. She'd not been able to get the moment out of her head. How the slight stubble on his jaw had scratched across her face. His soft lips, what his tongue had felt like stoking her own.

A shiver wracked her.

"I'm glad for it, cousin. I want to see you happy and settled, and Hamlyn will do as well as Oglemoore. More so, in fact, for he's richer and higher placed in society."

"Stop talking as the duke's daughter and seeing people for what they have and not who they are."

Clara laughed, taking no offense. "It is a hard lesson to unlearn, Olivia. And you're a duke's granddaughter, so the same as me. In any case, there is one thing that I wish to advise you of, caution you if I may, with Hamlyn."

"What is that?" she asked, eyeing his lordship for a second, or was it the third time since she sat down? A shiver of awareness thrummed through her at his dark, hooded gaze. He seemed to be listening to Oglemoore discuss the card game, but otherwise, his attention appeared solely fixed on her. She swallowed, unable to look away. Was he playing the besotted fool they had agreed to, or was there more behind the wicked, contemplating light in his eyes?

That Olivia could not answer, but she hoped it was both. That she wasn't so hideous and unweddable that she had to ask gentlemen to feign interest in her to make others take note.

"I adore Hamlyn, he is a good friend of the family and has been for some years now, but he is not without his faults."

His Grace had faults? Olivia doubted that very much. "Oh? What are his vices that you speak of?" she asked.

Clara lowered her voice to a whisper. "He has a mistress, Olivia. I feel I need to notify you of this should you look at him as a potential suitor. If he does offer marriage, at the end of my short house party or in London during the remainder of the Season, I need you to know this so you may put a stop to it before any vows are spoken."

Her stomach lurched, and she fought to school her features to one of indifference. So it was true. Hamlyn did have a lover. She closed her eyes a moment, ridding herself of the vision of them together. It was any wonder he kissed so well and knew how to make a woman dream with his devilishly handsome looks.

"I had heard a rumor, and will keep it in mind should anything progress."

"As you should," Clara continued. "He has had her for some years now. They are quite close from all accounts. Should you marry him, she must go. That is not negotiable in the contracts."

Olivia nodded. Even without her cousin's demands, such things could never stand. She would not marry a man who had a lover tucked away elsewhere. No marriage would stand a chance of being happy under such conditions. "Let me assure you, Clara, Hamlyn is being kind to me and nothing more. He has no intention of offering for my hand. We are friends." Disappointment stabbed at her at the truth of her words. She wanted the night over with and the sanctity of her room. "I'm going to retire. I shall see you in the morning." She stood. "Goodnight, everyone," she said to the room at large, slipping from the salon and making her way upstairs.

Not far from her room, footsteps sounded fast and determined behind her. A hand clasped her upper arm, whirling her about. Before she could say a word, Hamlyn took her lips. She stilled in his arms, shock rippling through her before other emotions took hold.

Pleasure. Need.

He was too delicious for words, even if she were capable of uttering any right at this moment.

His arm slipped about her waist, wrenching her against him. Her hands wrapped about his neck, her fingers tangling into the locks at his nape. His kiss was hot, deep, and wonderful. Her body burned, came alight like a flame. Unabashedly she pressed herself to him, the secret place between her legs undulating against his manhood that stood at attention.

He made a sound, half gasp, half groan. Did he enjoy her movements? Was this how men and women found pleasure? Was this what ladies of the night wanted every time they were in their lovers' arms?

He drew back, his breathing ragged, his eyes bright with need and something else she could not read. "Goodnight, Olivia," he whispered, and then he was gone, striding away without a backward glance.

Olivia stared after him, her body not itself. Her fingers touched her lips, still tingling from his kiss. What was he doing? She glanced up and down the hall, seeing no one else about, certainly not Lord Oglemoore, whom she was supposed to be flaunting her newfound friendship with Hamlyn with.

Why would the duke kiss her so?

She smiled, biting her lip before turning for her room. Perhaps his attention toward her was not wholly schemed after all. A sweet idea to mull on while she went to sleep, and if there was one gentleman who was pleasant to reflect on, it was Hamlyn and his wickedly handsome face.

CHAPTER 7

*O*livia sat at the breakfast table the following morning, disappointment threatening to make her lose her composure.

"I am terribly sorry to have to bring our house party to an end," Clara continued, "but we must travel up to Scotland without delay."

"I hope there is nothing wrong, Stephen," Olivia stated, knowing how close Clara's husband was with both his sisters.

"A difficult pregnancy, and I must be there for Sophie. She needs her family around her at this time. Her sister-in-law is in Edinburgh, you see, and therefore we have been summoned."

"We are sorry that our few days here will come to an end," Oglemoore said, standing and placing his napkin down with a flourish on the polished table. "We shall depart forthwith and hope to see you all very soon in town."

Hamlyn met Olivia's gaze, and she could see the regret in his eyes. He gave her a small bow. "Good morning to you all, and thank you for having us."

As the door to the dining room closed, leaving Olivia, Clara, and Stephen alone, as her friend Athol had opted to break her fast in her room, Olivia turned to her family, seeking answers. "Whatever has happened that has you racing to Scotland? I hope Lady Mackintosh is not in any danger?"

Clara reached out, taking Stephen's hand. "We have received word that there are complications with her second pregnancy. Nothing too serious, it is told, but it will be her last child. We need to be there for her. I'm sorry to have to cut our house party short, my dear."

Olivia shook her head, the house party be damned. "Lady Mackintosh comes before any silly house party. Do you wish for me to join you? I do not have to return to town."

"No, you should go and enjoy what is left of the Season. I will write to you and notify you of Sophie's progress and outcome. I'm certain we shall bestow good news on the birth of their child soon."

Olivia frowned. "If you're certain, I shall do as you ask, but you will be missed. Please give my love and good wishes to Lady Mackintosh and tell her that I pray for her every night."

"Thank you, dearest."

The remainder of the day was frantic. Trunks were packed, the house closed up, and by dusk, Olivia's carriage was rumbling into the streets of Mayfair. With both her parents long gone, she did not look forward to returning to the house on Grosvenor Square, the large, empty rooms, and quiet surroundings. Her companion, who had remained in London, stood at the door as the carriage rocked to a halt. A welcoming smile on her lips.

"Olivia, welcome home. I'm so pleased you've returned safely." She came down the steps, joining her. "I have taken the liberty of having your dinner ready. As soon as you're settled, I'll have it brought up to you."

"Thank you, Anna," Olivia said, entering the house. After Clara's marriage to Mr. Grant, she had grown closer with her companion Anna, and now they did most things together, going out to balls and parties. Anna, having lost her husband several years ago to a lung ailment, had sought employment.

"What a shame the house party has come to an end. When do you believe Lady Clara and Mr. Grant will return to town?"

"Not for several weeks, I would think." Olivia moved into the front drawing room, pulling off her gloves and bonnet. She sighed as she sat before the unlit hearth, pleased to be home. The night was warm, and already Olivia missed the clean and clear night skies over Kent. "I will see out the Season here alone, but we shall muddle along well enough. Athol will be in town next week. She had to travel back to her parents' house in Bath before coming here."

Anna seated herself across from Olivia, clasping her hands in her lap. "Were there any gentlemen at the house party who caught your eye? I understood Lord Oglemoore was present."

She sighed, leaning back in her chair. "Lord Oglemoore was present, but he showed scarce interest in me. More for my friend. There is nothing between myself and his lordship. He made that perfectly clear in Kent." The thought of his treatment made her tempered anger simmer to a boil. It was beyond time that the gentlemen within society who treated women like property suffered a set down or two. A good clip about the ears may help also.

"Well, now that you're back in town, perhaps he will explain himself. Seek you out and make amends. He was certainly showing considerable attention last year. I cannot see his lordship being so fickle as to treat you with so little respect as to cast you aside."

And yet, that is exactly what he had done. He had cast her aside in Kent and had made no pains to hide his affections for her friend.

"I shall enter society and finish the Season, but I think next year I shall return to Fox Hill. I feel at my age I'm no longer obligated to attend every year. And Fox Hill is my home, the estate my papa left me. I do not need a husband if I do not find one to my liking. I can become an old, unmarried maid and do well enough on my own."

Of course, she would seek out Hamlyn now that they were all returned and see if he would continue to help her. Oglemoore had been everything she'd wanted in a husband, but now he would rue the day he treated a duke's grand-daughter with no respect.

The image of Hamlyn's handsome features fluttered in her mind and erased all thoughts of Oglemoore. If only the duke were more marriageable material. He was not. He had a longtime mistress for starters and one whom she doubted he was ready to part with. The idea of his lordship taking his pleasure with a nameless woman made her want to snarl. Not that it surprised her his lordship would seek a woman away from the *ton* for his pleasure. He showed no interest in marriage or searching for a wife when she'd crossed paths with him last year, and never had she heard a rumor he was courting anyone in particular.

The memory of his kiss before her room at Chidding Hall made her stomach flutter. What a shame he was off the market, and his kisses were all for show and nothing more.

Olivia frowned as a light knock sounded on the door, a footman entering with a tray laden with food.

"Ah, your dinner is here," Anna said, taking it from the servant.

Olivia picked at her meal, thinking on her musings of Oglemoore and Hamlyn. She had marked Oglemoore simply because he'd taken a keen interest in her. The idea that she had thrown herself before an uninterested gentleman was humiliating.

Olivia shook the disturbing thoughts aside. She would finish off the Season with the help of Hamlyn and have retribution. No longer would she seek out Oglemoore, or try to keep the friendship she thought they had.

One day she would like to marry, have children, a family to call her own. The man she married would be loving and loyal, not fickle and false.

"The Davenport ball is tomorrow evening, Olivia. Do you wish for me to send a note to her ladyship to tell her you will be attending now that you're back in town?"

"Yes, please, Anna. That would be best, I think." Olivia finished her meal and wished her companion goodnight. The Davenport ball was as good a place as any to start her next phase in her plan, and there was little doubt Hamlyn would be there.

A smile quirked her lips at the thought of seeing him again. It was pleasant having a friend who knew her secrets, her wishes. That he had not denied to help her or teased her mercilessly over her plan helped her estimation of him.

With Hamlyn on her arm, one never knew. Other gentlemen may show awareness, and Oglemoore would be nothing but a passing phase, an apparition of her past before she stepped into her future. A mistake one was wont to forget.

CHAPTER 8

*T*he Davenport ball was a crush. The multitude of scents, perfumes, powder, and sweat that mingled in the air not always pleasant. Laughter and chatter overrode the possibility of quiet conversation. The only lovely feature of the ball was the music and the skill of the orchestra hired for the evening.

Olivia stood alone at the side of the room, content to watch the *ton* at play, Anna not far from her side. Couples danced, people drank champagne in abundance—a ball resembling the madness and gaiety of a night at Covent Garden more than a Mayfair dance.

She had not seen Athol here this evening, and she could only assume she had not returned to town in time to attend.

A tall gentleman who towered half a head over most present started her way, his golden, wavy locks giving her a clue as to who he was. She bit back a smile, unable to stem the hope that swelled within her that Hamlyn was here and had not forgotten their plan. Had not forgotten her.

He came before her, his eyes twinkling in mirth and pleasure. He bowed. "Miss Quinton. How pleased I am to see you here this evening."

She smiled up at him, giving him her hand. His lips brushed her silk glove, and the pit of her stomach fluttered. He was so handsome, and on seeing him yet again, she had to admit that perhaps he was even more handsome than Oglemoore. How had she not noticed him at a ball before now?

"I'm happy to see you too, Your Grace."

He pulled her toward the floor as the first strains of a waltz sounded. "Dance with me, Miss Quinton."

She chuckled, unable to refuse him and not wanting to if she were honest with herself. They made their way onto the floor, taking their places. Other couples stood about them, and with the crush of the night, it placed them closer than they ought to be.

The hem of her golden, silk gown touched his boots, and she was certain he could feel her heart pumping hard in her chest. His eyes raked her, taking in her dress, warming in appreciation. He swung them into the dance, and Olivia laughed, feeling as light as a feather in his arms.

"You look beautiful this evening, Miss Quinton. That gown is quite fetching."

She could not look away from his stormy, blue orbs. "You're very good at this game I have asked you to play, Your Grace. One would even think that sometimes you mean what you say, so proficient that you are."

He cocked his head to the side, pulling her close as he spun them at the end of the room. "What would you say if I were to admit to not playing your game? That what I say is heartfelt?"

"I would say you're lying, but I would enjoy the compliment in any case. A woman is never unhappy to be told she looks beautiful or fetching or something thereof."

His hand slipped lower on her back and pulled her ever

so slightly closer to him. The breath in her lungs hitched, and her body liquified. Hamlyn made her feel things she'd never felt before. A simple touch, like the one on her back, should not be enough to discombobulate her, but it did.

She had not reacted so with Oglemoore, and the knowledge gave her pause. She had liked Oglemoore, they had got along well enough, but she'd never wanted to kiss his lordship as much as she longed to kiss Hamlyn right now.

Olivia tore her gaze away from his lips, which were slightly tilted in a knowing grin. She met his eyes, and the hunger she read in his blue orbs sent her pulse racing. "You know it as much as I do you're the most handsome woman here this evening. Are you so blind that you cannot see every married and unmarried gentleman ogling you, wanting you? Men, no matter what they may say to disavow my opinion, are tonight jealous that you're in my arms and not theirs."

Hamlyn gestured to a place somewhere over her shoulder, and he spun her, giving her the ability to see what he had. "Look, Oglemoore is no different. He has been glaring at us both these past few minutes. I think you may safely say that his lordship is jealous of our association."

Oglemoore who? Olivia no longer cared about what Hamlyn's friend thought or decided. All she could think of was being in this man's arms—his secure hold, his height, and devilishly handsome face that was hers to enjoy. Savor.

"My plan would not have worked had I not too had one of England's most fetching rogues on my arm, making everyone envious. Do you not see the young women who flutter their fans when you pass, their mothers discussing your assets and worthiness for their daughters? If I am making men jealous, you too are making women equally so."

His eyes narrowed. He closed the space farther between them, and the breath in her lungs hitched. He would not dare kiss her here. Hamlyn may be a rogue, but he was no fool.

"It is fortunate then for you that I have you in my arms and not anyone else." He threw her a wicked grin, his thumb making tiny circular motions against her back. "How do you wish to play this game now that we're back in London? I cannot steal you away here and kiss you. Oglemoore will not be able to see."

The idea of Hamlyn kissing her made her yearn for him to do precisely that. It had been several days since she'd tasted those delicious lips that smiled down at her. Felt his hunger for her, to have more of what he could make her feel.

Her heart quickened, and she flexed her hand on his shoulder, reveling in the feel of his superfine coat beneath her palm. "You do not wish to kiss me in any case, Your Grace. You are a veritable tease, and you know it."

His chuckle was deep and laden with promise. "Would you care to walk with me and see if that is the case?" he whispered against her ear.

She shivered. What was this that he was doing to her? It was any wonder women fell at his feet, and he had kept his mistress so long. No sensible woman would want to lose a man as seductive and charming as Hamlyn.

"You would not dare. There is no point to us stealing away. It would serve no useful purpose with our plan."

He shrugged, maneuvering them close to the side of the ballroom floor. "No useful purpose, you are correct, but a pleasurable one when all told. Shall we?" He spun them to a stop, stepping back and holding out his arm for her to take.

Without thought, Olivia placed her hand on his arm and let him lead her out of the ballroom. They stepped outside onto the large, flagstone terrace. Other couples mingled out-of-doors, groups of guests spoke and drank champagne under the light of the full moon and lanterns that were hung from the wisteria growing on the trellis above.

After the cloying, overwhelming scent of indoors, the

purple flower's sweet perfume was refreshing. They strolled down the terrace, speaking to guests who turned toward them.

Hamlyn kept his hand atop hers, unfazed if his marked attention was noted. A footman passed them two champagne flutes, and His Grace handed her one, clinking the glass rims together.

"To the Season. May you gain what you're looking for, my sweet Miss Quinton, and have a happy heart."

She tipped her glass against his, unable to hold the smile his words brought forth on her lips. "You know, Your Grace, you can be quite the flatterer and a sweet man when you want to be. You speak of me and my unmarried state, but what of yours? You're what, one and thirty from what I hear? Do you not think a wife ought to be in your life sooner rather than later?"

He shrugged, sipping his drink. "Are you applying for the position, Olivia?"

Since the day of their kiss, he had not used her name, and to hear it on his lips now sent her wits to spiral. How lovely it sounded coming from him. She would never get sick of hearing it, she was sure.

"No, of course not, and you should stop your teasing. We're supposed to be tricking other people of our acquaintance, not ourselves."

"Hmm," he answered noncommittedly. "Very well, you are right. I'm not searching for a bride as yet, but that is not to say I shall never marry. I'm certain there is someone out in the world who will pique my interest, and I shall court her."

A pang of jealousy, strong and unexpected, tore through Olivia. She did not want to think of Hamlyn courting another woman and one he would promise to love and cherish for all time. It was almost as bad as His Grace having a lover tucked away in town.

"Ah, yes, but what will your mistress think if you start to court a woman? I should imagine she will be terribly displeased to lose your protection," she said, unable to hold back the words a moment longer. And wanting desperately at the same time for him to deny her claim.

CHAPTER 9

*J*asper sucked in his champagne and understandably choked. He coughed, his mind reeling at the knowledge that Miss Quinton, Olivia, knew he had a mistress. How on earth had the woman found out?

"That, my dear, is a conversation subject decidedly off-limits."

"What a shame?" She grinned, the gesture not reaching her eyes. She sipped her wine. "I know that if I were your lover, I would be terribly upset to lose you. There is something unique about you, Hamlyn, that I do not even think you're aware of."

"Really?" he asked, curious, the idea of having her as his lover an image he'd thought of quite a lot these past days. "Do explain, my dear."

"You're likable. Honest and trustworthy. Both men and women of our social sphere know this of you. It is why I trusted you with my plan to make Oglemoore madly in love with me again just to spite him. I know you will not abuse my trust in you and tell anyone of what we've spoken. I think you're a good person. A good friend to have. Your mistress knows you are not violent and would not mistreat her, so yes, I think she would miss you terribly should you marry and leave her to find a wife."

Jasper cleared his throat. "We should not be talking about my mistress." He took another long swallow of his champagne. "It isn't appropriate."

"Neither were our two kisses in Kent, but they still happened." She paused, staring up at him, her eyes narrowing as her gaze flittered over his features. "Would it be so terribly crass of me to admit that I would like to kiss you again?"

An ardent, uncontrollable need thrummed through him at Olivia's words. He glanced at the many people who surrounded them. He could not kiss her here, even though he longed to. He took her hand, pulling her toward the steps that led down to the lawn.

As idly and unhurried as he could appear, Jasper led Olivia deeper into the gardens. The Davenport's London estate backed onto a small, wooded area if his memory served him correctly. And he wanted them to be as far away from prying eyes as they could be.

All thoughts of showing his affection, his interest to the *ton* at large fell away. Jasper wanted Olivia alone, all his for a small piece of the night. The idea of Oglemoore seeing them no longer mattered, nor did her request to make his friend green-eyed.

Oglemoore could go hang. The thought of Olivia kissing his friend as he was about to kiss her heated his temper. He fisted his hand at his side, forcing the troubling thought aside. Oglemoore would not have her, not now and certainly not after he had discarded her without a second thought.

Who in their right thinking would not want Olivia in their arms? She was perfection, sweet and playful, not to mention absolutely stunning. He had seen how men devoured her this evening in her red, silk gown with gold beading across the bodice.

He'd almost swallowed his tongue at the sight of her. So beautiful, alluring, and unattached. Untouched by anyone. Never married or sullied by another man's hand. Simply perfect.

The need to have her in his arms, to taste her sweet lips once again, was overwhelming. He'd carved a path through the abundance of guests, needing to be by her side. He'd left Oglemoore gaping after him, barely saying good evening in his haste to be beside her.

His reaction to Olivia did send a small tremor of fear through his mind. He'd never behaved in such a way toward a woman. Not even his past lovers had he singled out as much as he had Olivia.

Was there more happening between them besides a deal, a prank on his friend to make him covetous? Was this more than his promise to Oglemoore that he'd keep Olivia distracted so he may court Athol and ask her to be his wife.

They came to the end of the garden, only dappled light from the terrace and the mansion behind them reached them here. He turned, gazing down at her.

Their eyes met. Held. Time stood still, his body thrummed with expectation and need.

"We're quite alone now, Hamlyn. It is highly doubtful Oglemoore will see your attention toward me out here in the bushes," she teased, amusement in her eyes.

He reached out, clasping her side and pulling her against him. She did not fight him, obliged his request. Her hands fluttered against his chest, and he wondered if she could feel his heart beating fast beneath his ribs.

It felt as though his organ would burst free from his body. The intoxicating scent of jasmine wafted in the air, taunting him further. He leaned forward, kissing her cheek, her jaw, until he found the lobe of her ear.

Her inhale of breath spurred him further. Her hands slid up his chest to settle and squeeze his shoulders.

"You smell good enough to eat, Olivia."

She shivered in his arms, and now all he could think about was eating her in truth, of lifting her siren-red gown to her waist, laying her over the nearby stone bench, and taking his fill. Bringing her to climax on his face, reveling in her sighs and begging as he made her come.

Holy fuck, he was in trouble.

He kissed her throat and groaned when she clasped his jaw in her hands, bringing his mouth back to hers and kissing him. God damn it, yes. This is what he wanted. Her, in his arms, kissing him with as much desire and need that catapulted through his body.

Her mouth fused with his, her tongue tangling with his own. The kiss was not sweet. It was hard, frantic, and had an edge of demand to it. It took ownership of him, and he was at a loss as to how to bring his senses back from spiraling.

He reached down, sliding his hand over one ass cheek that he declared the most perfectly taut piece of backside he'd ever held. He kneaded her thigh, lifting it about his hip, and pushed himself against her.

She gasped through the kiss, and he felt her undulate, taking what she could of him in this position. His cock, hard, grew to attention when she pressed herself to him.

Olivia mewled some unintelligible sound, but he understood her completely. He was as mad and as hot for her as she was him. All thoughts of his friend, of his plan to keep Olivia respectively occupied vanished.

Never in his life had he ever behaved without so much as a care when around an unmarried woman. He'd had many affairs, yes, but the women were widows, unhappy in their marriages, or were from the *demimonde*. Never the *beau monde*.

He did not need this complication in his life, but also he could not, would not, let Olivia go from his clasp. Heat rushed to his groin, and he knew he could spill in his breeches if they continued what they were doing.

Olivia seemed to have lost all thought too. She rubbed against him like a kitten seeking a pet. Her breath mingled with his, and he knew she wasn't far, could climax here and now in the gardens at a *ton* ball.

Jasper broke the kiss, let go of her leg, and stepped back. She stumbled before righting herself, staring up at him. Her eyes were as glassy as the moon, twinkling up at him like two bright stars that had found their purpose in the sky.

God damn it, he wanted to be her universe. He wanted to do whatever she asked him to. But he could not seduce her. Take her here and now in the garden like some rutting beast.

"Why did you stop?" Her question was breathless, and somewhat uneven.

It killed him to hear the need in her tone. He understood better than she would ever imagine what she was going through. However, there was one thing she would never know, and that was how close she came to being tupped in the outdoors at a grand London ball where anyone may be watching.

"If I do not stop now, there will be no turning back. It is not the deal we made, Olivia. We must try to remember that the next time we embark on kisses in darkened gardens where no Oglemoore will view my regard."

His words acted just as he wished, and like a bucket of cold water had been poured over her head, she stepped back, busying herself with righting her gown.

"You're right, of course. I'm so sorry." She laughed, and he did not miss the nervousness in the gesture. "You're very good at what you do, Hamlyn. You made me forget myself."

He had forgotten himself too. Utterly reprehensible actions he could not allow to happen again. He would show interest, court, and flirt with her in public, but he could not steal her away, be alone with her unless he wanted her for himself.

And he did not want Olivia, as precious and sweet as she was.

Truly he did not, he reminded himself.

He was not ready for a wife. His father had not married until his forties. He was one and thirty, too young to settle down to only one woman for the rest of his days.

She threw him a small, brittle smile, and a punch to the gut would have been less sharp. He swallowed, taking her hand and pulling her back toward the ball. Jasper did not look at her again, not even when he deposited her beside Anna, her companion, and bid them both goodnight.

Walking from the ball, he rolled his shoulders, feeling the burn of Olivia's gaze on his back. He was her friend, helping her make Oglemoore pay for his base treatment of her. What he needed was a good hard shag with his mistress.

Summoning his carriage, he tapped his feet, unease and annoyance thrumming through his veins. Charlotte would soothe his soul and scratch his itch. He climbed into the equipage, calling for Seymour street and forced himself not to look back at Davenport house.

CHAPTER 10

Three nights passed, and Olivia had not seen Hamlyn for as many days. Where was he? After their third kiss, she had watched him stride from the ball with a feeling of unease and uncertainty running down her spine.

She had not wanted him to leave and nor did she understand what had actually transpired between them. All she did know was she wanted to kiss him again and again. To have him hold her in his arms, tease her senseless and make her crave.

Never in her life had she wanted to act unlike the lady she had been brought up to be. She wanted him to touch her where she ached. To feel his large, erect manhood press against her sex. Take her as a man would take a woman, fill her and inflame her as much as she was already.

Oh dear, she had turned into someone she could not recognize.

Had he mentioned wanting her in that way, asking if she would permit him such liberty, Olivia was certain she would have allowed him to make love to her.

She'd been all but ready to lie on the grassy lawn and give him what they both wanted.

Her friend, having returned from Bath, stood beside her, sipping her ratafia. "I'm not certain that I want Oglemoore as my husband any longer. I went to the pump rooms while I was home in Bath, and I met with Lord Dormer. How handsome and accommodating he is. And," she said, pointing across the room, "do you see he too has returned to London? I think he is back to court me."

Olivia glanced in the direction of Lord Dormer, an earl from Derbyshire, and noted him nodding in welcome to her friend. "Is he not looking for an heiress? I thought I heard it said that his pockets are for let."

"They may be, but I'm more than capable of fixing his currency issue." Athol grinned. "He is handsome, do not you think?"

Olivia frowned. "What about Oglemoore? The last time we spoke, you were quite determined to have him as your husband, and you kissed him."

"That was in Kent, Olivia. Do keep up."

Taken aback, Olivia stared at her friend, wondering who she was or had become in the last few months. She turned, sipping her wine and watching the dancers who were partaking in a minuet. Across the room, she could see Lord Oglemoore talking with a group of gentlemen, his attention sometimes stealing over to where they both stood.

Athol, seemingly noting his lordship's notice, mumbled something about needing to go to the retiring room and disappeared into the throng. Oglemoore watched Athol leave, his eyes following her out of the room. Olivia had thought he would follow her, but he did not. Instead, he excused himself from his conversation and started toward her.

Olivia watched him, again agreeing with herself that

Oglemoore was a handsome gentleman, but now there were a few minuscule things she noticed that she had not before. He was shorter than Hamlyn, less refined, and had a pettiness about him she had not thought him capable of.

What man courted a woman for a Season, only to never offer for her? That was certainly how he'd treated her last year. His fixation on Athol at her cousin's house party made his conduct even worse.

"Miss Quinton," he said, taking her hand and kissing it. Where once Olivia would have reacted to his touch, to his presence, now she was merely bored. He bored her, and that in itself was telling.

"How nice to see you again. I see you returned to London safe and sound. Are you enjoying the ball this evening?"

She smiled, glancing about the room. "I am, my lord. Very much so." She gestured to where Athol had departed. "I'm sorry you just missed Lady Athol. She will be most displeased to have missed you."

He nodded, coming to stand beside her. "I shall, catch up with Lady Athol in good time, but it is you I wanted to seek out. Would you care to dance with me? I believe there is to be a waltz soon."

Olivia started at his request, not the least interested in taking a turn about the dancefloor in his arms. He continued to stare at her, seeking an answer, and she had no option but to concede.

"Of course, my lord. I would like that very much."

He smiled, and for a moment, neither of them spoke. Olivia fought to think of something to say. A conversation starter or the latest gossip going about London. Anything to halt the plainly obvious fact they had nothing to discuss.

"My friend, His Grace, the Duke of Hamlyn danced with you the other evening. I hope I shall too bring such joy to your night as he seemed to achieve."

Olivia stilled at his lordship's words. Did Oglemoore mean the waltz she and Hamlyn had shared or their kiss, that to this day made her toes curl up in her silk slippers? "The duke dances well."

Oglemoore chuckled. "Well, of course, he does, my dear. He has had the best dancing masters to teach him during his youth. A marquess I may be, but I still hope to do our dance justice this evening."

"I'm sure you shall, my lord. It is only a waltz, after all." She studied his profile as he sipped his wine. What was he up to? He had not sought her out at her cousin's house party. In fact, for a time there, Olivia was certain she had the pox or some other type of illness that would make her unpalatable to his lordship.

His interest in her yet again, hot and cold, was like a season gone topsy-turvy. Had her marked interest in the duke made Lord Oglemoore see her in a new light? Did he wish to court her again over her friend, who seemed less than interested in the marquess? She hoped that was the case so she could stomp on his emotions like he did her.

"I see Hamlyn has arrived. The ladies will be pleased," Oglemoore professed, a small smile playing on his lips.

At least his friendship with the duke did not seem affected even after Hamlyn played her game of making Oglemoore jealous. Olivia glanced over to where the duke was giving his regards to the host and hostess, bowing over her ladyship's hands.

"You've been friends with the duke for many years. How was it that you became acquainted?" She had not asked before, and they were an unlikely pair, having such different personalities.

"Hamlyn saved me from a bloody nose at Eton. I was not much liked for whatever reason. He stopped the Earl of Dormer as he is now from giving me a thorough thrashing for merely bumping into him during a change of class. We have been friends ever since."

So Hamlyn was also an honorable man and loyal. She liked him even more now knowing that about him. She glanced over to where she saw him last and caught him talking to Lady Graham and The Duchess of Carlton. Hamlyn took a sip of his brandy, and his eyes met hers over the rim of his glass.

From across the room, Olivia felt the reaction to his gaze. It smashed into her like a thousand horses toppling her to the ground. The glance was filled with promise, questions she was unsure she had the answers to.

After their kiss the other evening, something had changed between them. Certainly, the presence of Oglemoore at her side was not having the same response she had last year. In fact, he may not even be standing beside her for all she cared about the matter.

Was she a terrible person changing her mind so quickly on whom she wanted for a husband? She had been determined to marry Oglemoore. But his denial of her, his treatment in Kent had put paid to that thought. She did want him to regret his choice, but she would no longer entertain the idea of marrying him herself.

Oh no. And while she may not marry Hamlyn either, so long as she continued receiving his delicious kisses, she would be well pleased.

"The duke is a good man. You are fortunate to have him as your friend."

The strains of the waltz sounded, and Oglemoore bowed before her. "My dance, Miss Quinton."

She allowed him to lead her onto the floor and take their places. The music started, and then they were gliding about the room, another uncomfortable silence descending between them. What was wrong with her that she could not keep up a conversation with the man? Had her kissing Hamlyn stripped her of her wits when it came to other men?

Refusing to speak of matters that were wont to bore one to death, Olivia elected to remain silent and simply to enjoy the glide and steps of the dance. Oglemoore was well versed as a dance partner, but she may have been dancing with Athol for all the influence it caused in her.

No shivers of delight, no hunger for a man's lips to take hers, no desire to hear his voice whisper sweet words against the whorl of her ear.

They spun and moved beside and around the other couples, and all the time not a word was said. As the dance came to an end, Oglemoore swept her to a stop, smiling over her hand. "Thank you for the wonderful dance, Miss Quinton. I hope we shall partner again this evening."

Olivia thanked him, stepping off the floor only to run directly into a wall of muscle. She stumbled, and a pair of strong arms wrapped about hers, holding her steady.

"Did you enjoy your dance, Miss Quinton?"

Hamlyn.

His voice sent her nerves to jump, and she steadied her feet. She met his gaze, and had she hoped to see pleasure written across his features, she would be sadly disappointed. She schooled her emotions, wondering whatever she could have done to vex him.

"I hope I did not hurt you just then, Your Grace. I was not watching where I was going."

He humphed out a disgruntled breath before holding out his arm for her to take. She did not dare refuse him. He strode to the side of the room, away from the ballroom floor. "I suppose you were otherwise occupied dancing with Oglemoore. Our newfound friendship seems to be having the effect that you wished. He is taking an interest."

Hamlyn stopped and flicked his chin in a direction across

the room. Olivia looked to where he pointed, only to see Oglemoore watching them, a contemplative look in his eyes.

"Perhaps it is working," she admitted, not wanting to have Hamlyn leave her so soon should he think his work to gain her a husband served. That was no longer the case, not if she were honest.

Oglemoore was not honorable, nor likable now that she knew him better. Hamlyn, on the other hand, was a catch for any woman in England.

"How many more nights do you think you will need my help in securing him? Mayhap I ought to lean close to your side, like this," he said, dipping his head, the breath of his words kissing her neck. "So he shall think we're speaking secretively."

Olivia closed her eyes, reveling in his nearness. Having him with her again after three days was too long. She turned her head, placing her lips within a breath from his. His eyes dipped to her lips. Need thrummed between them.

Her stomach flipped, and for the life of her, she could not look away. "Where have you been these last days? I had wondered if you had changed your mind in helping me." Not that she wanted him to help her in that sense any longer. Oh no, now she wanted Hamlyn close to her for another selfish reason altogether.

Now she wanted Hamlyn by her side so she might have a chance with him. The man she had thought to use for her own means.

"I am not incensed," he replied, stepping back and giving them space.

Olivia looked about and noted a few eyes upon them, Oglemoore's too. "Yes, you are, or you would not be so curt with your answers. Is there something the matter? Has something happened that you're now so put out with me?"

A muscle worked in his jaw, and she could see he was

fighting to voice what was running through his mind. Dare she hope Hamlyn was no longer interested in making Oglemoore jealous any more than she was? Dare she hope he too was fighting the blossoming feelings that she herself was having?

"I have been busy elsewhere, that is why you have not seen me."

Olivia stared at him, not believing that for a moment. "Is that the truth?"

Hamlyn sighed, a muscle working in his jaw. "Oglemoore mentioned at Whites the day after the Davenport ball he had noted our dance and stroll on the terrace. I hoped that it would be enough for him to figure out who he wanted to marry. That I come here tonight and find you dancing with his lordship, hanging off his every word, I suspect my deliberations are right?"

They were not right, and nor was she hanging off Oglemoore's every word. She could not care a hoot what the marquess had to say. In fact, they had hardly spoken at all. "I think I shall need your assistance for a while longer, Hamlyn. Oglemoore spoke of Lady Athol, and so I do not think he's turned his attention back to me as yet," she lied.

Olivia, unsure how to react to Hamlyn's strange mood, fought to find the words to keep him from storming off yet again. His disagreeable nature this evening may not have anything to do with her. May, in fact, have something to do with his mistress or some other matter.

The thought made her blood run cold, and she fought not to glare at the guests in the room.

"So, I'm to help you still?" Hamlyn ran a hand through his hair, leaving it on end. "How much longer shall you need me to act the besotted fool? I'm not one to play such a character ever."

Olivia's attempt to remain cordial gave way to irritation.

She looked up at him, pinning him with a warning stare until he met her eyes. "You agreed to help me. Stop acting like a jealous fool."

"I am not jealous, madam."

She scoffed. "Then why are you talking to me as if you're angry with me for dancing with Oglemoore? As if you do not want to see me with him. That was the deal, was it not?"

"Damn it, yes, that was the deal," he seethed, taking her hand and pulling her from the room.

CHAPTER 11

*Y*es, God damn it all to hell it was the deal. And one he, after having arrived tonight, wanted to discard. Along with Oglemoore. He could bugger off as well.

Seeing Oglemoore clutching her and smirking as he danced with Olivia sent his temper ricocheting to heights he'd never experienced. Olivia was his friend, he reminded himself. He was the one who offered to help her tease Oglemoore into proposing marriage so she may spurn him in return. Instead, kissing her three times now had made his mind more muddled and unclear than it ever had been in his life.

Today, in fact, he'd gone to his see his mistress. He'd intended to spend the day shagging, taking her in as many ways as he could possibly think. Anything to clear his mind of a particular dark-haired goddess. Yet, instead, he had spent the time discussing the end to their understanding. The pension he would gift her that would see her settled comfortably for the rest of her days. Charlotte had been good to him, and he wanted to ensure she did not have to work or find a new protector if she did not choose to.

Now, at tonight's ball, without having fucked his afternoon away, he found his blood pumping hot and fast. Seeing Olivia in Oglemoore's arms had sparked his ire, and he could not seem to rein it in.

She was not for him. He did not want a wife. His reaction to seeing her be courted by another was preposterous. He needed to get a grip on himself.

"Yes," he ground out, "that was the deal. I would therefore appreciate it if you could hurry the hell up and make him offer for you before I lose my patience."

The moment he said the words, he wished he could pull them back. Shock registered on her face, and her eyes filled with unshed tears. Oh, God damn it. Now he'd made her cry.

In an instant, Jasper's annoyance and hurt—yes, it was hurt that he was also feeling—dissipated. He pulled her along the darkened passage farther from the ball and out of sight of the guests.

The muffled sounds of a quadrille played as he walked her along the deserted hall, far enough away from the door that they would not be overheard. "I'm sorry, Olivia. I did not mean what I said."

She tugged her arm free. Fear curled in his gut that he may have lost her friendship, acting like a cad. He liked her, more than he ever thought he would when he'd accepted her proposition.

"How dare you chastise me. You agreed to my scheme. I did not force you."

He ground his teeth, hating the idea of Oglemoore marrying the woman standing before him, wiping her cheeks with the back of her hand. He was a bastard, and he deserved to go to hell talking to her as he had done.

Fool.

"I do not understand the attraction you had for him, my friend or no. He chose another, played you a fool. Do you not want a marriage full of desire and love? An all-encompassing union you cannot get enough of? One that has respect above anything else?"

She sniffed, meeting his gaze. "Of course I do, and I will not accept anyone's offer of marriage unless I have all those things. I want Oglemoore to pay for his treatment of me, nothing more. He has not learned his lesson yet, I think."

Her words sent a frisson of hope to course through his blood. So, she wasn't so set on Oglemoore that she would dismiss *him* out of hand.

Jasper stilled at his own thoughts. Dismiss him? What on earth was wrong with him? He did not want a wife. If Olivia did not stand before him, he'd smack his own self about the ears.

He pulled her into his arms, running his hands over her back, giving comfort. "I did not mean what I said, Olivia," he whispered against her neck. Her slight nod of acceptance tore at his heart, and he kissed her shoulder.

Hell, she smelled divine, clean. Like a room full of hothouse flowers. They stood so close he could feel her chest rise and fall against his. The slight shiver that stole through her when his lips brushed her skin. Unsated, he took the small lobe of her ear into his mouth and suckled it.

Thankfully she wore no earrings, and it allowed him to tease her, kiss her as much as he wanted.

"You should not be kissing me, Jasper. This is against the rules we've just been arguing about, is it not? Your demand for our fake liaison to be over."

Oh yes, he wanted it over with, but not for the reasons she thought. He wanted her for himself. Having her in his arms again, having spent the past three days thinking of no one but Miss Olivia Quinton told him there was something peculiar about his attachment to the chit.

He knew what that regard was now. He no longer wanted to help his friend keep her away from him, so he may win Lady Athol Scott's affections. Oh no, holding Olivia now told Jasper that he wanted her in his bed.

The thought of her marrying another, being courted by anyone else, was like a stake to the heart, and he would not allow it to occur.

She pulled back, looking up to meet his gaze. "If you do not wish to continue with my plan, I understand. It does not mean that we cannot remain friends."

Friends? Oh no, no, no, that would never do. He wanted to be her lover and nothing less. "No more talking, Olivia." He dragged her against him, holding her face in his hands. "Kiss me," he begged, brushing his lips against hers. "Just kiss me and erase the memory of me seeing you in Oglemoore's arms."

She gasped, kissing him back. Her arms wrapped about his neck as her mouth slammed against his. It was hot, delicious, and hard. His blood pumped fast in his veins. He bent down, clasping her thighs and picking her up. She understood his motive and hooked her feet about his back. Her core pressed against his cock, hard and aching in his breeches.

Jasper closed the few steps to the wall and pushed her up against the silk wallpaper. She moaned through the kiss as he used the extra support to thrust against her heat. Stars burst behind his eyes, and he wanted to flick open his breeches, free his cock, and sheath himself in her warmth.

She moaned, pressing against him. "You make me want things I do not understand."

Oh, God almighty, she made him want things he never thought to want or need too. "As do you," he admitted, kissing her yet again, determined this time not to leave her longing for more, but to ensure she found pleasure from him and him only.

CHAPTER 12

Olivia was not herself, nor did she care where she was. Music continued to play somewhere in the house, laughter and clinking of glasses and plates sounded, but she pushed it all to the side, focusing on the man in her arms.

Concentrating on what that particular man was doing to her.

Her body burned, ebbed, and flowed with a need she could not sate. He was doing something to her, but what that was she could not fathom.

She clutched at his shoulders, scoring her nails into his skin as a tremble teased her most sensitive flesh. "I want more, Jasper. Please, help me."

He mumbled words that no well-bred woman ought to be privy to, and then she was standing again on her silk slippers, Jasper breathing ragged and hard before her. He looked like a wild man, unkempt and completely disheveled.

Olivia ran her hand through his hair, pulling it to bring him close for a kiss. "You are too handsome for your own good. Do you know that?"

His eyes burned into hers, and a wicked light shone back at her through his blue orbs. "The same could be said of you, Olivia."

And then she felt it, his hand, sliding up her leg and pooling her gown at her waist. He slipped his fingers between her legs, brushing his hand across her mons. She ought to feel embarrassed at his touch, push him away, mortified he dare touch her *there*, but she could not bring herself to care.

His fingers softly rolled a particular place, and her legs threatened to buckle. Olivia rested her head against the wall and gave in to his touch. What was he doing to her?

Bliss, utter, decadent pleasure rolled through her as he worked his magic touch against her flesh. Like a wanton she had not known she was, she parted her legs, giving him admittance.

"That's it, my darling. Open for me. Let me touch you."

Oh, she'd let him touch her as much as he liked if this is what he made her feel. Like her body was not her own. Taunting and teasing her toward a pinnacle she imagined quite wonderful, but wasn't for sure certain.

He kissed her, deep and long, all the while his touch never abated. He overwhelmed her, and she clutched at him, her only means of grounding, and then it happened. With each stroke of his hand, pleasure rocked through her body, thrumming at her core and bursting into light.

Olivia gasped his name, riding his hand like a woman outside of herself. All she knew was that she wanted more of what he had given her. Was not ready for this to end.

Where had Hamlyn been all her life, and why on earth had she taken so long to find him?

She slumped against the wall and knew she had a silly, self-satisfied smile on her lips. Olivia did not care. Jasper kissed her neck while he righted her gown.

"You're so beautiful. I shall never forget you coming apart in my hands, Olivia. You're truly magnificent."

Olivia opened her eyes, leaning forward to wrap her arms tighter about his neck. "I had no idea that such a thing was possible between a man and a woman. Can I do something similar to you to bring you joy?"

His eyes scorched her at her words, and she knew the answer to her question before he replied. "Oh yes, you certainly can, but not here. I should not have touched you in such a public place where anyone could have come across us. It was foolhardy of me."

She grinned, brushing her lips against his. "But so very worth it." And now that she'd done this once, she would do it again. Something told her there was more to know and enjoy in a man's arms, and she couldn't wait to find out what.

👑

*T*he following evening Jasper stood beside Oglemoore and fought to keep his patience with his friend. The man was becoming a menace, and not only that, a gentleman who he doubted knew his own mind.

"I thought you were going to ask Lady Athol for her hand in marriage? You're now saying that you're unsure who you want to be your wife?"

Oglemoore shrugged, sipping his wine. "Lady Athol, rumor has it, has been seen taking the air in Hyde Park with Lord Dormer. You know the fellow, the one who wanted to bloody my nose back at Eton." He shook his head, his lips thinning into a displeased line. "I'm unsure what her feelings are toward me now that we're both back in London."

Jasper schooled his features and bit back the words of telling his friend that karma was an unfortunate mistress and one that Oglemoore had obviously suffered from. He'd played Olivia last Season, threw her aside for her friend, and now had the same happen to him. Jasper ought to feel sorry for him, but he could not. After treating Olivia with so little respect, he could not help but be glad Oglemoore had missed out on both the women.

"I think you should stop our game with Miss Quinton. That will allow me the opportunity to court her during the last weeks of the Season. I'm certain she will be amenable to my interest, and should I ask her, I think she will marry me."

Jasper massaged his temple, trying to stop the incessant ache that thumped there. "You no longer want me to distract Miss Quinton away from you as I have been these last few weeks. What if someone else catches your interest in town, and you throw her over yet again? I do not think you should court Miss Quinton a second time."

Oglemoore gaped at him, clearly affronted. "And whyever not? She is not engaged or attached. You do not see her in a romantic light. The only reason you speak to her at all is because of my bidding. Do not tell me you've grown a conscience since I asked you to help me. That is unlike you, Hamlyn."

It may have been what he was like before he'd grown to know Olivia, but the thought of her being hurt for a second time by Oglemoore would not do. He would not allow his friend to play Olivia the fool no matter how many years they had known each other.

"Miss Quinton deserves better than being your second or third choice. Move on and find another to marry."

Oglemoore frowned, sensing Jasper's ire, which was simmering to a boil. "I will not play her a fool again. I promise you that, my friend." Oglemoore clapped him on the back as if all were forgiven, and Hamlyn was merely playing a protective father. He was not. In no way would he allow

Oglemoore to change his mind on a whim and think everything was perfectly well.

"I see Weston has arrived. I need to speak to him about his gelding he means to auction at Tattersalls. I may be interested in him if the price is right," Elliott said as he moved away.

Jasper watched as his friend moved off into the throng of guests. He narrowed his eyes, not caring for his words or his plans for Olivia. Jasper may have started out keeping Olivia distracted enough that she would not grow too upset about Oglemoore's attention toward her friend, but things had changed now. They were close, most certainly friends, even more than that.

He spied her across the room, smiling and chatting with the Duchess of Carlton. Oglemoore moved past her, certainly within her notice, and she did not glance his way or proceed to wish him a pleasant evening. Had Jasper been a betting man, he would have laid money she had not noticed his friend at all.

The thought pleased him, and he finished the last of his drink, a quiet calm settling over him that Olivia would not be so foolish as to allow Oglemoore another chance at winning her hand. Surely his time with her, even if she thought that time false due to their understanding, would make her see that not all men were the same. That there were men in the world who would like her for who she was, her kindness, sweet nature, pleasant self... Not simply because she was available, and it was time for the gentleman to choose a bride.

Olivia deserved to have a marriage of love. Anything less would be a waste of her life.

Later that night, he caught up to her as she was entering the supper room, thankfully on her own. He sidled up to her, dipping his head to ensure privacy. "Would you care to take supper with me, Miss Quinton?" he asked, reveling in the pleasure that bloomed on her handsome features.

"Of course," she gushed, coming to a stop behind the line of guests already waiting to choose their meal. "I did not know you were going to be here this evening. Did I not hear that you best Lord Lindhurst in a sparring match at Gentleman Jacksons, and he still has not forgiven you?"

Jasper laughed, remembering the day well. "Ladies are not supposed to know details such as those. Who told you?"

She shrugged, taking a plate from a footman and studying the selection of food laid out before them. "I forget who relayed the gossip, but he is, from what I understand, still quite put out. I'm surprised they allowed you entry."

"I'm the Duke of Hamlyn, there are few who would not admit me." Jasper picked up two crab cakes and a lobster tail. "He has asked for a rematch, and perhaps I shall let him win that bout, merely to keep the peace."

She turned with a plate laden with her selections. "That is very kind of you. I doubt I would be so charitable. I dislike losing as well, you know."

They made their way over to a table for two, seating themselves. "Is that why you asked me to help you with Oglemoore? Simply because you wanted revenge so desperately?"

She threw him a sheepish look. "In part, it was wrong of him to court me only to throw me aside when he deemed me not actually what he wanted. However, I do think that our ruse has paid off. He was questioning me at last night's ball, similarly to how he was toward me last year. I cannot help but think that Athol's disinterest in him since her return to town and your marked attentions toward me have reminded Oglemoore what he's thrown aside." She chuckled. "The poor man is wasting his time with me, I'm happy to report."

Jasper chewed his lobster, taking his time to cool his annoyance at Oglemoore's renewed attentions. "For what it is worth, I do believe you can do better than Oglemoore. He is my friend, yes, but even I am not blind to his faults. He should not have treated you the way he has. I'm sorry he hurt you."

A smile touched the corners of her lips. Her gaze bored into him, and he hoped it was interest for him he read in her eyes and not Oglemoore.

Heat licked his skin, and he had the overwhelming desire to reach out, touch her, anywhere, her hand, her cheek, a lock of hair, just so long as he was touching her.

"I no longer want Oglemoore, Jasper," she whispered, holding his gaze.

He took a calming breath, his heart pounding. What did that mean? "May I escort you home this evening?" To ask such a question was scandalous. He ought not, but nor did he want to leave her side. Jasper told himself it was to ensure she arrived home safely. She had no living parents and a questionable chaperone, so a gentleman ought to step up at times.

"That is kind of you, but you need not do that. I can catch a hackney home. It is not far in any case." She smiled, taking a sip of her champagne. "I could probably walk from here, all told."

He shook his head. "No, I could not allow that." Just the thought of her walking home sent a chill down his spine.

"When did you wish to depart?" she asked. "I am ready to leave whenever you are."

His body tightened at the thought of having her alone in his carriage. Five minutes or five hours, he would take whatever he could. "When you've finished your meal, we can leave. I'm at your service."

She raised her brows. "How delightful that sounds. I shall hold you to that, Your Grace."

He almost groaned. *Oh, please do.*

They finished their meal and separately made their good-byes to their hosts, before coming together on the front steps of the London home. His black carriage, pulled by two gray mares, rolled to a stop not long after.

A footman opened the door, and Jasper helped her up into the carriage. He called out the address before joining her. He sat opposite, waiting for the carriage to lurch forward before closing the blinds. If he had minutes only, he wanted to make full use of them.

Her eyes glistened in the dark, and it was only every now and then when they passed a street lamp that he saw her pretty face. He untied the blinds, letting them down.

"Why the privacy? Are you planning something, Your Grace?"

He opened the small portal near the driver's chair and told his man to drive about Mayfair. "If I were," he said, turning back to face her, "would you think bad of me?"

She shook her head, a small curl bounced across her shoulder. "No," she whispered, her attention snapping to his lips. She bit her own, and his body roared with need. Although uncertain what was happening between them, the game they started to play had morphed into something so much different.

So much more.

CHAPTER 13

The carriage rumbled down the street, the driver taking pains not to take the corners too sharp. Olivia did not feel like herself. The look in Jasper's eyes left her feeling as if there was something in the air, something about to happen.

Between them.

For herself, she wanted Jasper to take her in his arms, to touch her, kiss her, be with her as he was the other night at the ball. His steely gaze did not shift from her person, and by the time he did speak, she was squirming on the leather squabs.

"Thank you for letting me take you home this evening, Olivia. I will admit to wanting to be alone with you all evening."

Olivia bit her lip, having watched him all evening, wanting to be alone just as they were now. Never had she wanted to be with anyone as much as she had wanted to be with Jasper. Oglemoore was nothing but a figment of her past imagination.

She patted the seat at her side and smiled as he came to sit beside her without a word. Her breathing increased, and she all but sizzled with a longing for him to touch her. Unable to wait a moment longer, she closed the space between them, taking his lips in a searing kiss and giving herself what she'd coveted since supper.

He kissed her back, clasping her face and tipping her head to deepen the kiss. His hands moved over her body, where she could not say until they clasped her breast. She sighed, loving his touch. He kneaded one, rolling the nipple between his fingers.

Olivia pushed herself into his hands. This was what it was like to be adored, to be wanted. She could get used to being with a man in such a way, and not just any man, but Jasper.

"You drive me to distraction," he gasped, kissing her jaw, her neck, swift nibbles toward her ear.

"I want to feel you. Let me touch you, Jasper," she whispered. He slipped the bodice of her gown down, taking a moment to admire her. His eyes burned a path across her body before he dipped his head and paid homage to one nipple.

His tongue was beyond intoxicating. He lathed, kissed, and teased her pebbled flesh, liquid heat pooling at her core.

"You want to touch me, Olivia? Be my guest," he replied, not moving from her breast.

She slipped her hands down his taut, muscular stomach, reveling in the feel of his perfect physique. Her hand dipped lower still. At the top of his breeches, the bulging shaft of his manhood, erect and ready, pressed against the pants.

He felt well endowed, not that she had anything to compare him to, but surely not many men stood to attention in such a way. Swallowing her nerves, she slid her hand over his length, basking in his moan when she squeezed him through the fabric.

He was wide and long and as hard as steel. "I want to see you."

He released her breast with a pop. Already she missed his kisses on her skin, but she wanted to know more about him, see what she could do to him to bring him pleasure. As much as he had brought to her only last evening.

Olivia pushed him back against the squabs, fixing her gown before turning her attention to the buttons at the front of his breeches. He sat back, kept his hands on the carriage seat, and allowed her to do as she willed.

With a patience she did not think herself capable of right at this moment, she worked the buttons free. Her eyes widened at the sight of his impressive manhood.

She ran her finger along his length, following the rigid, blue vein that stood out. "So soft." Olivia licked her lips as a bead of pearly white liquid formed at the end. Thoughts of what he would taste like bombarded her mind. Images of her taking his rigid length and slipping it into her mouth.

She wrapped her hand around his manhood and stroked. He moaned, closing his eyes, his hands fisting against the edge of the seat.

"You're killing me, Olivia," he groaned, his whole body taut and still.

Without a whit of trepidation, she bent over him, taking him in her mouth, wanting to taste him, feel and give him pleasure. One hand fisted in her hair, guiding, pulling her up only to push her back down.

She liked his command, and she enjoyed the power she had over him like this. He bucked under her, his quick intake of air bolstered her attempt to please him. To make love to him with her mouth.

He tasted of salt, of musk, and man, a delicious combination. He pumped into her, taking his pleasure, and she did not pull away. There was something uniquely erotic about giving another pleasure while taking none. Even though having Jasper in her mouth made her hot and needy.

"Enough," he gasped, pulling her from him. "My turn, my darling."

Somehow in the small space of the carriage, he carried her to the other seat, laying her down. He rucked up her dress to pool about her waist, and then he was on his knees before her, his eyes glowing with wicked intent.

Olivia gave herself over to the sensation of him kissing her *there*. She no longer cared what sounds she made, or Jasper's moans that mingled with hers. He kissed her, flicked and teased her flesh until she was writhing in unabashed need. Oh, yes, this is what she wanted. This, his mouth, his delicious tongue that she was certain was magic.

It wasn't, of course, it was simply Jasper.

*J*asper worked his cock with his hand as he fucked Olivia with his tongue. He could not get enough. He was close, so close, yet he would not spend until she found her own release.

He teased her nubbin, licked, and suckled her tiny erect button. Her fingers tightened on his hair. Pain tore through his skull, adding to the pleasure as the first contractions spasmed from her cunny.

Jasper let himself go, stroking his cock painfully fast. They came together, and he moaned against her flesh, licking and kissing her as she rode his face to fulfillment.

For a time, he stayed where he was, resting between her legs as he gathered his breath. Her wet, glistening cunny teased him still, and before he moved, he took one last opportunity to taste her sweet self.

She groaned, her fingers sliding over his face to tip up his jaw to look at her. "You're a wicked duke, Jasper."

He grinned, helping her to sit before he moved back to his seat. His cock, still semi-hard, took a little maneuvering to get back in his breeches. Buttoned back up, he looked across the carriage and met her interested gaze.

"I would like to see that as well one day."

"See what?" he asked, moving to sit beside her and pull her into his arms. She lay on his shoulder, the carriage lulling them both after their exertions.

"I would like to see you take yourself in hand and climax. Will you show me sometime?" she asked, looking up at him.

Her beauty, rather disheveled, cheeks rosy from their escapades made his chest ache. "I will show you, yes. So long as you do the same?"

Her eyes widened, and she sat up. "Is that possible? Can I find such pleasure myself?"

He groaned, the idea of her experimenting when she returned home almost too much for his hot-blooded self. "You can, of course. It is the same for men and women. You are not told these delights by your mother, but they are as true as you and I sitting here, spent and sated."

A wicked glint entered her eyes, and he knew she would touch herself. Maybe not tonight, but soon. His cock hardened at the thought.

"I can agree to those terms. When can I see you again?" she asked, her hand idly running over his stomach, playing with his coat button.

"I'm to attend the Cavendish's dinner tomorrow evening. Come to my home under cover of darkness. I can meet you at the mews if you prefer?"

Olivia took only moments to think over his words before she nodded, resting back in the crook of his arm. "I will join you at midnight."

He kissed the top of her head, the hours until he saw her again already too far away. "I look forward to your company."

"As I, you," she replied. Her response ought to scare him, but it did not. If anything, it hammered home just how much she'd come to mean to him. How much he longed to be in her company and no one else's. Their game's stakes had changed, heightened, and he was powerless to stop it and nor did he wish to.

That, however, did give him pause. What did that mean, and where would this newfound obsession for them both lead? Jasper adjusted his hold on her. He supposed they would find out, and soon enough. Tomorrow night, in fact.

CHAPTER 14

The following evening Olivia snuck out of her townhouse and made her way on foot to Jasper's home. She turned down the darkened alley beside his house, seeing the lights of the mews at the back of the estate. A shadowy figure of a man waited near the garden gate, and her steps slowed as she tried to make him out.

Trepidation marred her every step with the knowledge of what they would do this evening. Her being at the duke's home meant one thing and one thing only. When he had asked her to come, Olivia knew what he was asking of her, and she was powerless to say no.

She wanted to be with him in all ways. To have him make love to her, take her and make her his, even if for only one night. Although she was unaware of what her being here meant regarding their future, she did know she would never regret her choice.

He stepped from the gate, and the moonlight illuminated his handsome features. Her stomach did a flip, and she grinned, excitement thrumming through her blood. Tonight would be fixed in her mind for the remainder of her days.

At the age of seven and twenty, she was more than ready to be tupped. If she did end her days as a spinster, at least she would have this one night in his arms.

"Olivia," he whispered as she came up to him. He hoisted her in his arms and kissed her soundly. The fleeting embrace was not enough and only teased her for what was to come. She shivered, reveling in all that he gave her and clutching him close, having missed him since she'd seen him last evening.

"Come, I have champagne and oysters prepared in my room. We shall have a feast before I feast on you."

She let out a breath, already feeling the thrum of need he brought forth in her. "I would not think you would want any more food. How was your dinner at the Cavendish's?"

"Uneventful and the food unfortunately tasteless, although I do believe that was because my mind was occupied elsewhere."

He led her through the gardens, slipping them into the house by the terrace doors. Without being seen, they climbed the main staircase, making their way toward the ducal suite. Olivia had not known what to expect from Jasper's home, but she was surprised at the light, homey, and well-appointed rooms that encompassed the home.

The walls were adorned with light wallpapers and family portraits. There were flowers arranged throughout the common areas and the home smelled of springtime. His hand tightened on hers as they came to a set of double doors. He turned to her, meeting her gaze. "Are you sure, Olivia? There is no turning back from here."

She hoped he was correct in that estimation. Olivia reached for the door handle and opened the door herself, pushing it wide. Without a word, she pulled him into the room, locking them away from the world, his staff, society's expectations, everyone.

To hell with all that nonsense. Tonight, she would sleep with a man, give her whole mind and body to pleasure, and the consequences be damned. She'd worry about them tomorrow.

They stared at each other. The tension in the air wrapped about her, expectation and need riding hard on her heels. She stepped into his arms, taking his lips.

He wrapped his arms about her, reaching down to her bottom and hoisting her up in his arms. His steps ate the short distance to his bed. He kneeled on the mattress, laying her down. Olivia calmed her breathing as he rolled her onto her stomach, his hands running up along her legs, kneading her bottom before unbuttoning her dress.

"Jasper," she gasped as he kissed her neck, his fingers frantically working the laces of her corset, and then she was on her back again. With a wicked light in his eyes, he pulled her dress from her, her corset and shift gone.

His eyes darkened with need, and she squirmed, her breathing ragged as he simply took his fill, his eyes running hungrily over her naked form.

"So beautiful." He lifted her foot, sliding his hand along her silk stocking, only to pull it slowly off. She shivered at his touch, his ability to quicken and slow their undressing.

Olivia reached up, pulling at the knot on his cravat. "Now it's my turn."

"Not yet," he teased, standing and stripping without shame. His jacket, waistcoat, and shirt discarded on the floor. In his haste, a button flittered to the floor, his breeches wrenched down without heed to pool at his feet.

Olivia felt her mouth open at the sight of him naked. She'd never seen a man in such a state before, and certainly, this man, who stood before her, was the epitome of absolute beauty.

Rippled muscles stole across his abdomen, a light sprinkling of hair on his chest. His manhood was erect and large. Heat stole between her legs wet and aching.

She bit her lip, wanting him inside her. The need that thrummed through her stole any trepidation she had at being with a man for the first time. He would not hurt her. He would only bring her pleasure.

Olivia reached for him, and then he was there, over her, kissing her into blissful oblivion. His manhood teased her aching flesh, and she could not wait. She had spent years hoping, wanting a husband, a lover. The time for respite was over.

Olivia reached down and took him in hand, taking the opportunity to feel him again, tease and stroke his flesh. She placed him at her entrance, liking the way he felt there.

"I do not want to wait any longer, Jasper."

He stared down at her, almost nose to nose. "Tell me to fuck you. I want to hear you say it."

She sobbed, not wanting to play such a game and unsure of what the word he wanted her to state meant, but she could gather the significance of it. Olivia wrapped her arms around his back, scoring her nails down his spine.

"Fuck me, Jasper." She gasped as he thrust into her. Sensation swamped her, stinging pain, yes, but also fulfillment, pleasure, an ache that wanted to be pet and teased until satisfied.

He moaned her name, kissing her. Olivia lifted her legs, wrapping them about his back as the small hurt subsided, and then there was nothing but pleasure, satisfaction left in its place. She moved with him, pushed, and strove to reach the pinnacle he'd given her every other time they had been together.

This, however, making love, was different. It was coarser, harder, felt as though she would split in two if he did not make her come.

"Jasper," she gasped when he pulled out, flipping her onto her stomach and hoisting her bottom into the air.

"Stay like that," he commanded, pushing on her back when she went to sit up. "Trust me."

A shiver stole down her spine as he bent over her, kissing her neck and spine. And then he was there again, entering her from behind, filling and inflaming her more than she thought she could bear. She moaned as his deeper penetration teased a special little place inside.

She was going to die from the pleasure of it all. However would she live without this, without Jasper, when their game was over? She knew she could not.

*J*asper thrust into Olivia with a desperate need he'd never felt before. He wanted to fuck her in every way he knew. She rode his deep, long strokes, fought for her own pleasure, and he'd almost spilled his seed multiple times as her hot, tight cunny wrapped about him like a glove.

The slap of skin on skin was music to his ears. His balls tightened, pulled up hard against his cock, and he knew he was close. Olivia's muffled moans into his bedding told him she was as well. He increased his pace, hard, deep thrusts, and then she was there, grappling for purpose on the bedding, moaning his name as she convulsed around him.

"Fuck, Olivia," he panted, letting himself go. He pulled out, spilling his seed over her ass and up her back, using her sweet cheeks to drain him of his pleasure.

He collapsed beside her, and she turned, grinning over to him, a self-satisfied smile on her lips.

"That was utterly wonderful," she sighed, shuffling over to lie in his arms.

He pulled her close, dropping a kiss on her nose. "Let me catch my breath, and we'll go again."

She slid up against him like a purring cat. "You can do that again? I fear I shall never leave your bed, should you be so clever."

He chuckled, rolling her onto her back and settling between her legs. His cock twitched, working its way to being hard yet again. "Oh, yes, I can do that again and more. Just you wait and see."

"Mmm," she replied, wrapping her legs about his back. "I like the sound of that."

Jasper groaned when she pushed her wet heat against his cock, making him see stars. He liked the sound of it as well as he thrust inside her a second time in as many minutes, losing himself in her and not caring if he never found himself ever again.

CHAPTER 15

One week later, Olivia sat with Athol in her front drawing room that overlooked Grosvenor square. Her friend all but bounced in her chair, excited with some news she wanted to impart. What that news was, however, Olivia had yet to determine as she'd not stopped fluttering about and ensuring everything was perfect before she told her.

"Athol, tell me this news. We're alone now, and you have tea and biscuits just as you asked."

Athol beamed at her from her seat. "It is the best news, Olivia dear. I am engaged. Lord Berry has offered me his hand, and I have accepted him."

Olivia remembered to smile. At the same time, she tried to hide her shock. "I did not know Lord Berry had taken such a keen interest in you. I thought you had spent time with Lord Dormer when you were in Bath, and do not forget Lord Oglemoore."

A light blush rose on her friend's cheeks before she waved Olivia's questions aside. "Oglemoore has been long over, and Lord Dormer offered to Miss Wilkins last week. Where have you been, Olivia dear? Surely you heard that news during one of your nights out."

Olivia sipped her tea, having missed all of this news. The past week had been spent sneaking over to Hamlyn's home, spending countless hours in his arms and bed. Enjoying every kiss and touch he bestowed on her. He was a magnificent lover and one she would struggle to walk away from, now that she'd tasted what being with a man like him was like.

"Olivia, did you hear me? Are you ill? You're splotchy and red," Athol said, placing down her half-eaten biscuit on the small table before them.

"I'm quite well, the day is warmer than I dressed for."

"Well, are you not pleased for me? I am the happiest woman in the world."

Olivia smiled. "Of course I'm happy for you, dearest, I'm just startled, that is all. I have not heard of Lord Berry's affections toward you before this day. Are you certain he is the gentleman for you?"

Athol started at her words, a small frown between her brows. "Of course, he is for me. Are you not happy for me? I know that you have not found a gentleman to marry this Season, but I would have thought as my best friend you would be pleased for me, not jealous."

Olivia stuttered to form a reply. "Athol, that is unfair. Of course I'm happy for you, but you must admit that you've flitted about from Oglemoore to Dormer and now Lord Berry. It does leave one somewhat turned about."

"I thought you would be pleased." Athol stood, hastily pulling on her gloves. "It leaves Oglemoore free for you now, as you've always wanted. You may think I did not know that you preferred him. And certainly after your disappointment, which you hid unwell in Kent, told me that was the case. You may marry him now, and all will be well." Athol walked to the door before turning to face her. "That's if the marquess chooses you to be his wife."

Olivia stood, biting back the tears that threatened at her friend's harsh words. "It is no lie I thought Oglemoore was courting me last Season, and when I heard of him joining Clara's house party, I did hold a small hope that perhaps he would offer for my hand if his feelings were still engaged. But it has been many weeks now that I have not sought his company or his offer. I want nothing at all from Lord Oglemoore just as you do not."

"So you *are* angry and upset with me because he chose me over you, and that is why you cannot be happy for Berry and me. I shall take my leave of you, Olivia, and wish you a good day."

Olivia watched as her friend flounced from the room without a backward glance or apology. She slumped down onto her settee, lost for words. What had just happened? She had not meant to criticize her friend's choice, but to ensure she was happy with her decision. Marriage was forever, after all. It was not a decision one ought to make lightly.

A knock sounded on the door, and she gasped, glancing up to see Mary, the Duchess of Carlton, smiling in greeting. "I hope I'm not interrupting you, Olivia. I thought I would call by. I'm out and about making calls, and I saw Lady Athol leave rather suddenly, and I wanted to make sure everything was well."

Olivia stood, going to the duchess, and pulling her into the room. "You're always most welcome, Mary. Come, we shall have tea."

They settled down on the leather settee, the duchess studying her most peculiarly. "What happened between you and Lady Athol? You seem out of sorts to me."

Olivia sighed, handing the duchess a cup of tea. She rubbed her forehead, a slight ache across her brow. "She is recently engaged to Lord Berry, and I merely asked if she was happy with her choice. She's been so unsettled, allowing different men to court her that it is hard to keep up. She accused me of being jealous."

"And are you jealous, my dear?" the duchess asked, meeting her gaze over the rim of her teacup.

"Of course not," Olivia denied. "I am truly happy for Athol, but only several weeks ago she was kissing Lord Oglemoore. One week ago, she was being courted by Lord Dormer. One must admit to being skeptical of her decision making."

The duchess chuckled, setting down her teacup. "Let her have her choice. If she chooses worse than you would have picked for her, that is her own doing. And talking of gentlemen admirers, what is new with you, Olivia? How is the Season progressing?"

Excitement thrummed through her, and she shivered at the thought of Jasper. His touch, his kisses, his body that made her burn and come apart into a thousand stars. She would not see him tonight for they were attending different events, but tomorrow she would, and she was already counting down the time until they assembled.

"The Season has been quite diverting this year. What with Clara's house party to break up the time, and with only a few weeks left in town, I have enjoyed myself immensely."

The duchess nodded, a small smile playing about her mouth as if she knew something Olivia did not. "I have noticed Hamlyn is spending a great deal of time with you lately. To me, he seems quite taken with you, my dear."

Did he? She schooled her features, not wanting to burst out into childish laughter at the idea he liked her as much as she was starting to fear she liked him. They had not discussed their original deal for several days now.

Would Jasper pull away from her if she raised the possibility that her request of him had gone too far? That for her, spending time with him, getting to know him in all ways, not just the façade he portrayed to the *ton*, but the man behind the door when they were alone and private, had made her heart his. Or would he declare, as she hoped, undying love for her and ask her to be his wife?

She was not certain what she would do should he still be playing her game and had no emotional attachment to her at all.

"The duke and I have become friends, yes, but I'm uncertain of his intentions toward me. He has certainly not asked me to be his wife."

"Do you think he may?" Mary asked, a contemplative look on her pretty face.

Olivia shrugged, wishing with all her heart he would. "I do not know. That is yet to be seen."

"Hmm," the duchess said, her eyes narrowing. "I heard that he has parted ways with his mistress, and with his considerable attention toward you, which has not gone unnoticed in town, I wondered if there was something between you or if not, perhaps will be very soon."

He had parted ways with his mistress?

Olivia did not know how to answer such a statement, and for the duchess to bring up a duke's lover was far from appropriate. Not that Olivia could say much on the subject of appropriateness after what she had been taking part in the last week. Nights of debauchery and utter unadulterated pleasure.

"I do not know anything about the duke's private life, Your Grace. But if he does choose me to be his wife, of course I would hope he would part ways with his mistress. I would expect nothing less."

"Of course you wouldn't, my dear. Just know that should

you need any advice or guidance, I am in town and here to help you until your cousin returns."

"Thank you," Olivia said, seeing the duchess off only a few minutes later. She slumped against the front door after her two visitors for the day, both of whom brought up issues that were taxing and hard to discuss.

The duchess was right however, she needed to know where this love affair with Jasper was heading, if anywhere at all. She could not remain his lover forever, the risk was too high. And she was an unmarried woman, she didn't even have the cover of being a widow to protect her. Should the *ton* find out about their escapades, she would be ruined forever and her marriage chances along with it.

They needed to end the affair or marry. Those were the only two options. Olivia pushed off from the door, heading upstairs to bathe and prepare for the ball. At least tonight, she could dance and enjoy her time in the *ton* and not worry about talking about such matters with Jasper. Their conversation would keep for another day until she saw him again. A small reprieve this day at least.

CHAPTER 16

The widow Lady Craven's ball was a crush, but thankfully the late Earl Mayfair's home was generous enough to host such an event.

As expected, Olivia had not seen Jasper here this evening, and yet she had seen Oglemoore, moving about the room and talking to acquaintances since his arrival, not an hour before.

The Duchess of Carlton was also in attendance and had raised her glass of champagne in salute when they had spied each other across the room.

Olivia stood speaking with some friends when Oglemoore appeared before her, dipping into a bow. "Miss Quinton, how well you look this evening. Will you do me the honor of dancing with me?"

She smiled, offering her his hand out of politeness. Certainly her interest in the man had long ceased. In fact, as she placed her hand into his, she had to wonder what she ever saw in the gentleman. He had nothing on Hamlyn, who was amusing, kind, and sweet. Oglemoore had proven himself to be flippant, and after his treatment of her in Kent, she ought not to give him the time of day. Athol was fortunate to be rid of him, truth be said. There was something about the man that left Olivia knowing he would not be faithful or a true husband to any wife. She doubted he would part with his mistress if he chose to marry.

His lordship stumbled with the steps, and she shot a look at him. "Are you well, my lord?" she asked, moving forward with the dance.

"Of course." He chuckled.

She studied him a moment and noticed for the first time his glassy, unclear eyes. Was he foxed?

"A misstep, nothing more," he continued.

They resumed the dance, Oglemoore making so many errors they caught the eye of some of the guests. Not willing to be gossiped or mocked, Olivia falsely tripped and, feigning a sore foot, allowed Oglemoore to escort her from the floor.

A footman went to pass them, and his lordship reached out, snapping up two flutes of champagne, handing her one.

"Tell me, my lord, what are your plans once the Season comes to an end? Are you for Surrey?"

He finished his drink with barely a breath, and Olivia stared at his empty glass. The dance was not so taxing that one drank to such an extreme. "I'm not certain as yet. Everything is to be appointed." His slow, standoffish drawl piqued her interest.

"Is something the matter, my lord? You seem offended."

He started to laugh. Cackle would be a better term to describe his mirth. Other guests glanced in their direction before moving away from them. Olivia felt the kiss of heat on her cheeks.

"Nothing is the matter, my dear. Nothing at all, except..." He smiled, his mirth not reaching his eyes. "I do wonder what you're playing at, my dear. What you hope to achieve."

"Pardon me?" she asked, lowering her voice, not wanting anyone else to hear his accusations.

"Pardon you indeed," he replied, hiccupping. "I know you wanted me to marry you, had your heart set on an alliance with my family. I also know that out of spite, you turned Athol away from my suit, and now she is lost to me forever."

"I never did such a thing," she stated, her voice stern. "How dare you accuse me of such a thing."

"Athol told me herself. Tonight, in fact, stated that she has chosen another because you did not approve. How could you?"

Hurt spiked through her heart at her friend's lie. Why would Athol say such a thing? "I never turned Lady Athol from your suit. That she chose Lord Berry is perhaps more to your inability to ask her for her hand than anything I have done."

"You don't say?" he stuttered, stumbling toward her. "Well, I have some news for you, Miss Quinton. I have seen you these past weeks since Kent throwing yourself at Hamlyn. Flaunting your assets so to turn his head, but it is all a ruse, you know. He is not interested in you at all."

Olivia stilled, swallowing the bile that rose in her throat at his words. A ruse? Fear curled about her heart, and she looked around, not wanting to cause a scene. "I do not understand what you're saying. If you'll excuse me."

"I will not," he said, clasping her arm and holding her in place when she went to flee. "I knew you wanted me as your husband. I made a judgment of error last year in seeking you out to be my bride. I did not find you attractive as a husband should find his wife, and therefore I cooled my friendship with you once I realized my mistake. I asked Hamlyn on our way to Kent to keep you occupied and out of my way so I may court your friend. He readily agreed to keep you distracted. You were only ever a game, my dear. I hope you did not get your hopes up too much. I would hate for us both to have lost in love this year." Oglemoore smiled as if he were doing her a great service.

"You lie," she said, not able to imagine all that she'd shared with Jasper to be false. He could not act so heartlessly. Not even a rogue like he was.

Olivia stumbled back, catching herself on a nearby guest. She thanked them before fleeing, fighting her way through the throng of guests to the door. She could not stay here, did not want to listen to any more of Oglemoore's cruel words.

Jasper had only shown an interest in her at his friend's behest?

Oh dear heavens, she'd made a fool of herself. She had also made a fool of herself to Hamlyn. He knew of her plan to make Oglemoore jealous, and all the while, he was keeping her engaged for Oglemoore?

How could he?

Her vision blurred, her stomach roiled. Blindly she ran out onto the footpath, calling for the first hackney she spied, yelling out the direction to home. She had to leave London. Hide and never come back after this. The people at the ball would have heard Oglemoore and his cruel, mocking words. By tomorrow she would be the latest *on dit*.

She would never forgive Jasper for this. At least she had been truthful in her plan, and although she schemed to make Oglemoore jealous, she never intended to play anyone the fool as they had her.

The bastards had not done the same.

👑

Jasper sipped his coffee in Whites the following morning, reading *The Times* and thinking of tonight when he would see Olivia again. Yesterday he'd taken the time to go to the jeweler to have the ring his father had given his mother upon their engagement cleaned and polished.

Tonight he would offer Olivia his hand and his heart and hope like hell she would accept him. Their game, their original scheme to make Oglemoore jealous had not worked. Even though it was a lot of fun, it had changed, grown into something so much more than a game.

He adored her. Wanted her to be by his side for the rest of his life. His partner and wife. His love.

A hand came down over his paper, ripping it away. Marquess Graham glared at him, taking a seat across from him without a word.

"Graham, whatever do I owe the pleasure?" he asked, straightening his paper and wondering why he'd gained the ire of one of his friends.

"Indeed," Graham drawled, his mouth set into a displeased line. "Have you looked around you this morning, Hamlyn? Have you noticed anything different in your world?"

Jasper laid the paper on his knee and glanced about the room. The older gentlemen sat and ate their breakfast, drinking their coffee without a by your leave, while the younger men superstitiously glanced at him, raised their brows, and smirked.

He frowned, dread coiling in his gut. Whatever had he done now?

"You need to call out Oglemoore for making a fool of a woman who is practically family to me last evening. She was belittled and mocked and is now the laughing stock of London."

"What?" Jasper bolted upright. "What did he do to Olivia?"

Graham's jaw clenched. "Well, at least I'm glad to know that you assumed it to be Olivia who had been harmed." He paused. "Oglemoore, well in his cups last night, declared to anyone within hearing distance of his booming mouth that you had courted Miss Quinton only to keep her occupied and out of his hair. Made her sound like a besotted idiot toward the fool and a game for you and Oglemoore. How could you do that to her? She does not deserve such treatment."

Fuck!

Panic seized him, and for a moment, he could not speak. Could not think straight. "He said that to her?"

"Of course, and other things too. Cruel words that have seen her flee London. She will not return this Season, and you need to make this right. You have been seen on multiple occasions in her presence, dancing and paying attention to her every word. You will offer her your hand and declare Oglemoore a liar. Friend or not, I will not have Miss Quinton come out of this game you decided to play being the one to lose. You will be her husband, and she will save her reputation and pride. I do not care if you wish to marry her or not. That is what you will do."

Jasper would not normally take such a set down, such rules from anyone, but in this case, he would. He had already decided to offer for Olivia. He would not let her down in this. Face this scandal alone. "I will go to her and make things right." He would first find Oglemoore and give him a good dose of reality and possibly a fist to his nose.

How dare he tell Olivia of his plans? Why would Oglemoore have wanted to hurt her so?

He stood, throwing the paper onto the chair and striding from the room. His carriage waited outside the club, and he called out Oglemoore's address. Anger thrummed through him at his friend's treatment of her. The bastard would not come out of this smelling like a rose. He would make sure of it.

A few minutes later, the carriage rolled to a halt before the modest townhouse. Jasper took the stairs at the front of the house two at a time. He did not wait for the door to be opened, trying the handle himself and finding it unlocked.

The house was dark, the curtains yet to be opened even at this late time in the morning. A footman skidded to a halt in the foyer. "Your Grace, Lord Oglemoore has not yet risen today. Would you like to leave a message for his lordship?"

Jasper started up the stairs, ignoring the servant's calls for him to stop. "I shall wake him myself. No need to trouble yourself," he called out over his shoulder. The house was smaller than his own, and it did not take him long to find Oglemoore's room since his door was ajar, and there was a decidedly loud snore emanating from the space that reeked of sweat and spirits.

"Oglemoore," he yelled, slamming the door wide.

Oglemoore stuttered awake, sitting up. His once-friend blinked, his eyes narrowed as he tried to focus on one point. "Hamlyn?"

"Get up," he commanded, waiting for Oglemoore to slip from the bed. The man, still clearly foxed, stumbled before righting himself.

"Why do I have to get out of bed?" He glanced at the clock on the mantle. "It's not half past ten. A bit early for callers surely."

Jasper walked over to him, shaking his head. "This is not a pleasant visit between friends. I just did not want to belt you in the nose when you could not fall back on your ass." He pulled his arm back, made a fist, and cracked his friend in the nose. A satisfying thwack rent the air.

Oglemoore flew backward, falling onto his back, holding his nose and groaning.

Jasper rubbed the bones on his knuckles, a small cut on his skin from his assault. "How dare you treat Miss Quinton with so little respect. I shall never forgive you for being so cruel."

Oglemoore sat up, pinching the bridge of his nose to stop it bleeding. "I'm cruel? She turned Lady Athol away from me, and now I have no one. She was spiteful and did it to pay me back for not choosing her."

Jasper shook his head, striding to the door before turning to face his old friend. "You're a fool. Anyone with a brain could see that Lady Athol is as fickle as they come. She never cared for you, you idiot, but Miss Quinton did. A foolish mistake on her part, and now you'll be lucky to have her as a friend. What you did last evening crossed a line."

Oglemoore struggled to stand, swiping at his nose to wipe the blood from his face. "What does it matter to you? You were only pretending to help me. You're just as complicit in my hurting of her as I am."

"I'm to Kent now to talk to her. Apologize on both our behalf and hope that my friendship with her can be saved."

Oglemoore scoffed. "Do not tell me you have fallen for the chit. She may be rich and handsome enough, but is she worth losing our friendship over? If you chase her down, do not include me in your apology. I care nothing for her now that she has ensured the woman I intended to marry is lost to me."

"Olivia never did anything of the kind. You're just as blind as Lady Athol. Always looking for something you believe to be better, more handsome, more flirtatious, rich, or higher on the social rank. Nothing will ever be enough for either of you. It is just a shame you did not win Lady Athol, for you would have made both your lives a living hell."

Jasper strode from the room, ignoring the startled faces of Oglemoore's staff as he passed them by.

He slammed the front door to the townhouse, closing that part of his life along with it. His friendship with Oglemoore was over, and now he had to find Olivia and see if he could win back her trust and, dare he say it, affections.

Jasper called for home. He would win her back, earn her trust and forgiveness. They were suited in all ways. She made him laugh, love, and play with the utmost pleasure. He could not live his life without her in it. His future would be a bleak landscape should she refuse him. A missed opportunity that in time they both would regret, he was certain of it.

CHAPTER 17

*O*livia arrived at her estate and told her staff to inform all visitors she was not at home. She had been at her house for three days, and still the humiliation, the devastation that Lord Oglemoore's words brought forth in her were enough to make her cry.

Perhaps her playing a small trick on Oglemoore had forced karma to make an appearance. Still, the fact Jasper had been in on Oglemoore's scheme hurt. She had thought herself in love with the man.

There was nothing else left to say on the matter. She had fallen in love with him the moment she gave herself to him at his home. Never would she have been so careless unless a small part of her believed Jasper loved her in return and would make her his wife.

How desperate everyone must think her. What a pathetic human being. No doubt all of London was having a jolly good laugh at her expense right at this moment.

She stepped off the terrace in the twilight, walking out onto the lawns and toward the lake just visible through the trees. The water always brought on a calming effect, and she needed that more than anything right now.

"Olivia?"

She gasped, turning to face Hamlyn, who strode toward her, his steps as determined as the look on his face. What was he doing here?

"Leave, Your Grace. You're not welcome here," she said, marching back toward the lake and ignoring his calls for her to stop. She would never stop being angry at him. What he had done had made her look the fool. All this time, he knew of her plan while working for his friend. She cringed, her stomach threatening to bring up her dinner at the thought of it all.

"Stop. Olivia, wait."

She heard him running, and she took a calming breath, not wanting to listen to a word from him. Never again did she even want to see his two-faced mouth.

He caught up to her, clasping her hand to pull her to a stop. She wrenched free, startling him. "Do not touch me, Hamlyn. Do not ever touch me again."

The pain etched on his face pulled at the place her heart once beat, but she thrust it aside. Reminded herself what he'd done. What he and Oglemoore had schemed.

"I'm sorry. I'm so sorry, Olivia. Oglemoore was wrong to tell you what he did. His scheme was never meant to hurt you, merely let you down gently without him having to tell you outright that he did not want to offer marriage."

His words hurt, stung, and she crossed her arms over her chest. "How hard is it to be honest? I'm a grown woman, I can listen to a great many things and not get emotional."

"I know that," he said, tipping his head to one side, willing her to forgive him with his sad, worried frown, but she would not. She'd been humiliated in front of the *ton*. There was no forgiveness for such a slight.

"Oglemoore should have told you the truth. Hell, I should have told you the truth, but when you asked me to tease him into thinking he'd made a mistake, I decided another path. I enjoyed spending time with you, and if you found out Oglemoore was indeed courting another, and the game was over, I feared you would push me aside. I did not want to lose you."

"You did not want to stop tupping me is what you ought to be saying. Well," she said, starting for the pond once more, "you will not be touching me again ever, so I hope your game with Oglemoore was worth your time."

"Damn it, Olivia, listen to me." He clasped her arm, pulling her around. "I saw no harm in doing either Oglemoore's bidding or yours. When you seemed to lose interest in Oglemoore I thought it a blessing that perhaps you liked me more than your own game. My courting of you may have started at the behest of my friend, but it is not why I continued once we returned to London. I wanted to be with you. I enjoyed your conversation and wit. At someplace along the way, I wanted you for myself."

Olivia stepped back. He wanted her for himself? "Pardon?"

"I'm in love with you, Olivia. I traveled here as soon as I found out what had occurred in London. Since yesterday morning, after being denied entry for the second day in a row, I have been hiding in your woods. I hoped to catch you in the garden, and it wasn't until tonight that my luck changed."

Olivia watched as Jasper's lips moved, explained how he came to be here, but her mind had halted thought at the five words he just admitted. He was in love with her?

"You're in love with me?" she repeated, hating to sound so arrested.

He sighed, running a hand through his hair, stepping closer. "I am utterly, absolutely, wholeheartedly in love with you." He rummaged in his coat pocket, pulling out a small blue velvet box. "I had planned on giving this to you the night we were to meet again, but I suppose now is as good a time as any." He opened it, and she gasped, stepping back.

A diamond circled by dark-green emeralds twinkled up at her in the twilight. She met Jasper's gaze, unable to fathom what was happening. She was angry with him, she reminded herself. Had promised all sorts of retribution against his person, some of which may have involved torture. His asking to marry her had not been in her mind.

"Marry me, Olivia. I adore and love you so very much. You have my heart, and I do not want to be parted from you again. Please tell me you'll be mine."

Not quite ready to forgive him, she crossed her arms to stop herself from reaching for the stunning ring. "If you marry me, you do know that you'll be the butt of all jokes in town for marrying a woman who is the latest *on dit*. Are you proposing to save my reputation? Because I'd rather not have you if that is all my marriage will be, another falsehood."

"No." He reached for her, wrapping her in his arms. For a moment, Olivia thought about trying to escape his grip, but then, being in his arms again was a comfort that she'd missed these past three days. "While I do care about what people think of you, I also do not care what they think of my proposing. I know that I'm asking because I want you and no one else. Oglemoore is right at this moment sporting my opinion of him on his face, and I want you to show what I think of you on your finger. I'm the Duke of Hamlyn, no one would dare speak a word of Oglemoore's ploy against you from this day forward."

She narrowed her eyes, and yet, at his words, a little of her ire left her. "The *ton* will laugh at me, behind my back. I cannot return to London."

"I will blacken everyone's nose should they dare speak a word of Oglemoore's scheme."

Olivia debated hating him still, but at his earnestness, his soulful eyes, she could not. She reached up, wrapping her arms about his neck. Oh, how she had missed him. The thought that he was lost to her had broken her soul in two, never to be the same again.

"Are you telling me that Lord Oglemoore is donning a broken nose?"

He grinned, kissing her own nose. "And perhaps a couple of black eyes."

Olivia chuckled, and Jasper stepped back, lifting the velvet case yet again before her. "Will you marry me, my love? I promise you this is no lark. I want you to be my wife, my duchess, my lover and friend. Be mine?" he asked her, taking the ring out and holding it before her.

Olivia bit her lip, hope, love, and relief pouring through her like a balm. She held out her hand, smiling. "Yes, I will marry you, Jasper."

His smile lit up the twilight, and he slipped the ring on. It was heavy and so beautiful. Olivia stared at it a moment, unable to comprehend she was engaged. And not only engaged to be married, but to a man whom she loved so much that at times the emotion had almost overwhelmed her.

He wrenched her into his arms, spinning and kissing her. She clung to him, taking his lips, having missed him so very much. The idea of not being with him as they now were had torn her in two, and she had wondered if she would survive the heartbreak.

"I need you. Please tell me I can escort you back to the house?" he asked, his voice a gravelly, deep growl that promised unfettered pleasure.

"You may," she said after he set her down. She pulled him toward the house at almost a run.

*O*livia took Jasper directly to her room, shutting and locking the door on anyone who may disturb them. They stripped before the bed, only stopping to help the other with ties or clips they could not handle themselves before falling onto the mattress.

Jasper kissed her deep and long, relief pouring through him that she was his. That she had agreed to marry him and be his from this day forward. He would never allow anyone to insult or harm her again. He'd been a fool to have allowed his friend his stupid scheme. When he had the chance, he should have told Oglemoore to man up and be honest with Olivia.

Her legs wrapped about his waist and, unable to wait a moment longer, he took her, thrust deep into her welcoming heat, and made them one.

"Oh, Jasper. I have missed you," she gasped, throwing her head against the bedding as he took her with long, hard strokes.

"I missed you." He breathed in her delicious scent of jasmine and another that was wholly her. To think he could have lost the love in his arms through his own foolish actions left him grappling for purpose.

He would never hurt her again or embarrass her in such a way.

He took her lips, kissing her and slowing his strokes, wanting to make tonight last, take their time in making love, enjoy the other without time restraints. He would stay here forever if he didn't want to get her down an aisle within the week.

She shifted beneath him, seeking her own pleasure, and

he saw stars. Damn it, she made him want to lose control, to let her use him for her own means. Jasper reached down, clasped her ass and rolled, pulling her to sit atop him.

Olivia stared down at him, her eyes wide with uncertainty. "This is just another way in which to make love, my darling. Use me at your will," he offered, folding his arms behind his head.

She slid down on him, her exhale of breath making his cock harden to rock. She soon fell into a steady rhythm. Jasper breathed deep, steeling himself not to come. Her breasts swung before him, and she clutched at his chest, rising and falling with abandonment as she sought release.

"You're so damn beautiful," he gasped, reaching for her hips and helping her fuck him.

She moaned, throwing her head back, her long, dark locks tickling his balls. She convulsed around his cock, pulling him into such a strong, pleasurable orgasm that his moans intertwined with hers.

Her rocking upon him dragged his release out for longer than he thought possible. He could hardly wait until he took her again. She was an addiction he would forever crave.

She slumped over him, their bodies still engaged, and gasped for air. "Oh, Jasper. How lucky am I that I can have you in this way whenever I please?" She waved her ring before his face. "Tell me, when can we be married?"

"Return to London, and we shall be married by special license by the week's end. I cannot be without you in my life or bed another night."

"Mmm," she said, placing light kisses across his chest. "Yes, I agree. I do not want to not be there either." She grinned down at him, and his heart thumped hard. "I love you too. Just in case I had not said so already."

He pulled her close, rolling to lay over her. "I'm glad to

hear you say it, my love. I would hate to be the only one here in love."

She reached up, clasping his jaw. "You're not alone, and nor will you ever be alone again."

"Perfect." He kissed her soundly, catapulting them into pleasure a second time in as many minutes. The night was young, and there was more indulgence to be had, both in each other's arms and with each other's company—the unspoiled way to end the day.

EPILOGUE

One year later

True to his word, Jasper married her before the week was out in a small church in London. The Marquess and Marchioness Graham, along with the Duke and Duchess of Carlton, their only witnesses.

Twelve months on and Olivia still had to pinch herself every now and then to remind herself she was indeed married to Jasper, the Duke of Hamlyn, and absolutely, utterly in love with the man.

As promised, the *ton* did not dare gossip about her. Anyway, the *ton* had more than enough fodder to keep them busy after her friend Lady Athol married Lord Berry only to run away with Lord Oglemoore to the continent a month later. London had talked of nothing else, and Olivia had not heard from Athol since the day they argued.

All she could hope was that her friend was happy and not

regretting her choice, which seemed to change as much as the days of the week.

Now back in the country after a whirlwind Season, Olivia was glad to be at the ducal estate for the winter. Over the past weeks, she had grown severely tired and lethargic in the mornings, her stomach roiling at the oddest smells.

So much so she had sought out her doctor in town, only to have confirmed her most dearly wished-for dream. She was pregnant, and they were going to have a baby.

Olivia strode into the ducal suite, locking the door behind her when she heard the splashing of the bath. Striding into their bathing suite, Olivia made short work of her clothes, the amused, naughty light in Jasper's eyes telling her he did not mind that she was about to join him.

She stepped into the copper tub that sat before a fire, ignoring the bit of water that splashed over the sides. "Good evening, Your Grace. I have missed you today," she said, moving onto his lap, sliding her hands up his chest.

His own clasped her waist, moving her to straddle his legs. "Hmm, I have missed you as well," he said, kissing her lips, her cheek, her neck before nibbling on her ear. She shivered.

"I need to talk to you about something," she managed to say as he continued to tease her.

"Hmm, you do?" he said, his hand coming about to clasp her breast, kneading it. She gasped when his fingers rolled her nipple. "Does that feel good, wife?" he asked.

"Yes, you know it does, but let me talk first, and then we can play. I want to tell you something."

He leaned back, meeting her gaze. "What is it? Is something wrong?"

"Nothing is wrong, but there is something." She shook her head, wanting to dispel his unease. "Everything is absolutely fine. But you know how I have been so very tired of late, somewhat low-spirited and ill."

"Yes," he answered cautiously. "I have noticed," he admitted, his hands idly running over her back.

"Well, I know what has been ailing me of late."

Jasper frowned, his ministrations on her skin halting. "What is it? Should I be concerned?"

She shook her head, swallowing past the lump in her throat. So many months they had tried for a baby, and each time she bled, she had felt the stab of disappointment, the loss of a small part of them that she so desperately wanted.

"No, not worried. I think you'll be happy." She blinked back tears, and Jasper's frown deepened.

"Tell me, Olivia. You're scaring me now," he demanded.

She ran her hands over his jaw, reveling in the feel of the stubble there. "I'm pregnant, Jasper. We're going to have a child."

His eyes widened, his mouth moved, and yet nothing came out. It was a first for him. He normally had so much to say. "You're *enceinte*? Oh my, darling. You scared me half to death."

She laughed as he pulled her into his arms, more water sloshing to the floor. "My darling, darling wife. How happy I am. And are you sure," he said, reaching for her stomach and laying his palm over her there, "that you are well, and nothing is wrong?"

She shook her head. "The doctor suggested rest and healthy eating, no lifting of anything too heavy. Other than that, there is nothing to report."

He kissed her, long and slow, and her stomach fluttered. "I adore you so much. You will want for nothing, pregnant or not. I shall wait on you hand and foot."

She laughed, having lived with him for a year now, there was scant she ever had to do. He pampered, loved, and spoiled her beyond what was necessary at times. Now that she was having his baby, she knew he would only grow worse with his mollycoddling, but she would allow him his way. If it made him feel better, what harm did it do?

"I had started to worry that we may not be able to have children. I hope it's a boy, Jasper," she said, covering his hands on her stomach with hers.

"Whatever it is, I just hope that you are well, along with the baby. That is all that matters."

And seven and a half months later, Olivia did give birth safely. To a girl and a boy, and the duke was yet again in awe of his wife and spoiled her appropriately for the remainder of their days.

As he should.

Thank you for taking the time to read *A Duke's Wild Kiss*! I hope you enjoyed the fifth book in my Kiss the Wallflower series.

I'm forever grateful to my readers, so if you're able, I would appreciate an honest review of *A Duke's Wild Kiss*. As they say, feed an author, leave a review! You can contact me at tamaragillauthor@gmail.com or sign up to my newsletter to keep up with my writing news.

If you'd like to learn about book six in my Kiss the Wallflower series, *To Kiss a Highland Rose*, please read on. I have included chapter one (unedited) for your reading pleasure.

TO KISS A HIGHLAND ROSE

KISS THE WALLFLOWER, BOOK 6

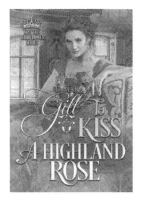

Available Dec 7, 2020
Pre-order your copy today!

CHAPTER 1

Edinburgh – 1810

he first week of the Scottish Season was a crush, and it was wonderful. Lady Elizabeth Mackintosh had to admit that being back within society's bosom with all the scandalous goings-on that occurred was just what she needed. It had been so long since she'd traveled away from her brother's estate, taken part of the gaiety her friends were forever reminding her she was missing. With a bountiful glass of chilled champagne in her hand, she inwardly toasted her unmarried friend, Lady Julia Tarrant, for making her attend tonight. The weeks to come would be filled with laughter, fun, and perhaps marriage if she were lucky enough to find a suitable husband.

The sound of a minuet filled the room. Unable to look away, Elizabeth watched the throng of dancers, one of them her good friend, Lady Georgina Dalton, a widow, who seemed exceedingly happy with the man holding her in his arms all but float about the dancefloor. He was very dashing, a little rakish even if the wicked gleam in the gentleman's eyes was any indication.

Married twice and sadly widowed the same number, Elizabeth would have to congratulate Georgina on having the man fall at her feet and so early in the Season. Now, if only introductions could be made for her, with a suitable gentleman who piqued her interest, the night would be perfect indeed.

"Well, well, well, would you look at that fine specimen of a gentleman? Too delicious to be English, don't you think?" said her friend Julia, her gaze fixed on the man across the room.

Elizabeth laughed, taking her arm. Julia, Georgina, and Elizabeth had their Season in London the same year and had formed a close bond ever since. Of course, this was helped by the fact that they were all Scottish by birth, heiresses, or had inherited their family's estates.

"Georgina certainly seems smitten by him. He's too dark-haired to be Scottish. Maybe Spanish, he certainly has eyelashes long enough to be European."

Julia nodded slowly. "Yes, and everyone knows a person's nationality can be guessed by how long one's eyelashes are," she teased.

Elizabeth grinned, not missing the sarcasm in her friend's tone. "Of course they can, silly. Did you not know?" The gentleman in question glanced their way, and Elizabeth quickly looked elsewhere, not wanting to be caught ogling him like a pair of debutantes. But what were friends to do when one was dancing with such a dashing gentleman other than to look and admire.

Julia sighed. "Well, it seems the Spanish fox has caught his hare for the evening, and you must agree, Georgina does seem very taken with the gentleman."

"You said Georgina was very taken with another such gentleman last evening. I no longer hold any sway with your words. You're a terrible tease." Elizabeth smiled, taking a sip of her champagne. "And what about you? Is there no one here tonight that has caught your attention? You cannot remain unmarried forever. There must be a man somewhere in Scotland who's perfect for our Julia."

"No one here, I'm afraid, is exciting enough to marry, but the Season is young and many more nights before us, perhaps my luck may change. And let's not forget, my aunts have threatened to travel here should I not become betrothed before returning home, so I must find someone. If at all possible, I would prefer someone ancient, who'll pass away within the first year of marriage, and I'll not have to bother with husbands after that."

Elizabeth laughed, having forgotten Julia was constantly trying to calm and beguile her two aging aunts. They thought their charge needed their help in all things, including gaining a husband. "So very true, I shall look about and see who's elderly enough to be suitable."

They both were quiet for a moment, watching the play of guests when a pricking of unease slid down Elizabeth's back. She gazed about the room, wondering what it was that had a shiver steal over her. "Should we move away from the windows? I think there's a draft here."

Julia nodded, and taking Elizabeth's arm, they headed to the opposite side of the ballroom. After a few moments at their new locale, the sense that someone was watching her wouldn't abate.

A gentleman bowed before them and asked Julia to dance, which she agreed, casting a grin over her shoulder as she went.

"Good evening, Lady Elizabeth."

The deep English baritone sent a kaleidoscope of

thoughts through her mind, of summer days full of laughter and love, of long walks and passionate kisses that would threaten to curl her toes in her silk slippers.

"Do I know you, my lord? I do not believe we've been introduced."

"That's because we have not. I'm Sebastian Denholm, Lord Hastings. It's a pleasure to have your acquaintance, my lady," he said, bowing before her with more deference than was needed.

The English Earl everyone one was talking about this Season here in Edinburgh. "And you know who I am? How?"

He leaned conspiringly close. "Doesn't everyone know who you are?"

Elizabeth started at his reply, knowing only too well what he hinted. It was no secret in the society they graced that she was unlucky in love. In London, all her friends had married around her. One after another during the Season, they were courted and whisked down the aisle before she had time to change her gown. Not her, however. She had been the good luck charm for those looking to wed, but the elusive gentleman for her seemed to be lost. "I beg your pardon, Lord Hastings, but I do not understand your meaning." She would not let him throw her disastrous past Seasons in her face. No matter how handsome he may be.

"I remember you on your coming out in town. London deemed you a good luck charm for debutantes looking to marry. I see you have not been caught by such inducement yet, my lady."

Heat suffused her face. She'd fought hard to forget the many young women who only befriended her so they could find husbands. It was the oddest situation and one reason she was attending this year's Season in Scotland. Even so, it did not look like she could escape those who attended from southern locales and who remembered. "How gentlemanly of you to remind me of the title. Is that why you're speaking to me now. Do you hope that your nearness to me will equate to you falling in love and marrying?"

He grinned down at her. "On the contrary. I have no interest in marriage just as it seems you do not."

Elizabeth fought to close her mouth that she was sure was gaping at him. Did he mean that by being by her rendered him safe? Was she so inapt to find a husband that the gentlemen now thought her a secure woman to be around? How absurd! Not to mention humiliating. She turned, facing him. "Let me assure you, my lord, that by being by me does not make you safe from marriage. I'm sure since I seem to be a lucky charm to the women of my acquaintance, it would also work on the men who flock to my side. You would be no different."

"Do many men flock to your side, my lady? Or am I the only one?"

She narrowed her eyes on him, unsure where his questions were leading, if at all anywhere. Why was he near her if he was not interested? He seemed to be playing with words and her to an extent. She did not like it. "You are beside me, are you not? I'm certain you will not be the last to grace my side this evening."

"I sought you out not to tease you, my lady, and I do apologize for bringing up your London Season. I merely wished to introduce myself and inform you of some news that I'm sure you will be well aware of soon enough."

"Really? What is this news you wish for me to know?" Vaguely she remembered his lordship from town, a rake who enjoyed the demimonde and widows more than the debutantes. Handsome as sin, rich and wealthy like many of her acquaintance, but always the same. Men who looked for the next thrill, the next piece of skirt they could hoist. Not marriageable by any length. No matter what anyone said, rakes did not make the best husbands.

"You inherited Halligale, I understand."

"I did," she replied. Her brother had gifted it not long after his marriage to Sophie Grant. He had wanted her to have a home close to him, but that was all hers. That is came with an abundance of land was equally generous. Her brother was simply the best person she knew.

"So, we're neighbors. I'm at Bragdon Manor," he continued.

She stared at him a moment, not having known that. If Lord Hastings was a Bragdon, he was closer than her brother was at Moy Castle. "I did not know you had inherited."

Pain crossed his lordship's face, and a little of the teasing light dimmed in his eyes. "I inherited the estate after my brother passed."

"I'm sorry for your loss," she said, automatically reaching out and touching his arm. The moment she did, she knew if for the mistake it was. Shock rippled up her arm, a bolt of some kind she'd never experienced before. Beth stepped back, breaking her hold.

"Thank you. My brother was a good man if not ruled a little by vices that others sought to their advantage." His lordship seemed to shake off his melancholy and turned, watching her. He had dark eyes, almost gray, the blue was so stormy. A very handsome man and one who knew that fact very well.

"We shall see each other often then," she said, sipping her champagne and willing her heart to stop beating fast in her chest. He was merely a man. A gentleman like no other. There was no reason her stomach would be all aflutter with him at her side."

He picked up her hand, kissing her gloved fingers. His

eyes held hers, and again her skin prickled in awareness. *Oh, dear.*

"I have traveled all the way from England, Lady Elizabeth. I intend to see you as much as you will allow." With a wicked grin, he turned and strode off into the throng of guests, leaving her to watch him. Her gaze slid over his back before dipping lower. Well, it was not only his eyes that were handsome, and what did he mean by his words? For the first time since her debut ball, excitement fluttered in her soul. Finally, perhaps this year, she would find love and have a marriage as strong and as sweet as her brother had found.

Maybe rakes did make the best husbands after all.

Want to read more? Pre-order To Kiss a Highland Rose today!

LORDS OF LONDON SERIES
AVAILABLE NOW!

Dive into these charming historical romances! In this six-book series by Tamara Gill, Darcy seduces a virginal duke, Cecilia's world collides with a roguish marquess, Katherine strikes a deal with an unlucky earl and Lizzy sets out to conquer a very wicked Viscount. These stories plus more adventures in the Lords of London series!

LEAGUE OF UNWEDDABLE GENTLEMEN SERIES AVAILABLE NOW!

Fall into my latest series, where the heroines have to fight for what they want, both regarding their life and love. And where the heroes may be unweddable to begin with, that is until they meet the women who'll change their fate. The League of Unweddable Gentlemen series is available now!

THE ROYAL HOUSE OF ATHARIA SERIES

If you love dashing dukes and want a royal adventure, make sure to check out my latest series, The Royal House of Atharia series! Book one, To Dream of You is available now at Amazon or you can read FREE with Kindle Unlimited.

A union between a princess and a lowly future duke is forbidden. But as intrigue abounds and their enemies circle, will Drew and Holly defy the obligations and expectations that stand between them to take a chance on love? Or is their happily ever after merely a dream?

TO VEX A VISCOUNT

TO DARE A DUCHESS

TO MARRY A MARCHIONESS

LORDS OF LONDON - BOOKS 1-3 BUNDLE

LORDS OF LONDON - BOOKS 4-6 BUNDLE

To Marry a Rogue Series

ONLY AN EARL WILL DO

ONLY A DUKE WILL DO

ONLY A VISCOUNT WILL DO

ONLY A MARQUESS WILL DO

ONLY A LADY WILL DO

A Time Traveler's Highland Love Series

TO CONQUER A SCOT

TO SAVE A SAVAGE SCOT

TO WIN A HIGHLAND SCOT

Time Travel Romance

DEFIANT SURRENDER

A STOLEN SEASON

Scandalous London Series

A GENTLEMAN'S PROMISE

A CAPTAIN'S ORDER

A MARRIAGE MADE IN MAYFAIR

SCANDALOUS LONDON - BOOKS 1-3 BUNDLE

High Seas & High Stakes Series

HIS LADY SMUGGLER

HER GENTLEMAN PIRATE

HIGH SEAS & HIGH STAKES - BOOKS 1-2 BUNDLE

Daughters Of The Gods Series

BANISHED-GUARDIAN-FALLEN

DAUGHTERS OF THE GODS - BOOKS 1-3 BUNDLE

Stand Alone Books

TO SIN WITH SCANDAL

OUTLAWS

ABOUT THE AUTHOR

Tamara is an Australian author who grew up in an old mining town in country South Australia, where her love of history was founded. So much so, she made her darling husband travel to the UK for their honeymoon, where she dragged him from one historical monument and castle to another.

A mother of three, her two little gentlemen in the making, a future lady (she hopes) and a part-time job keep her busy in the real world, but whenever she gets a moment's peace she loves to write romance novels in an array of genres, including regency, medieval and time travel.

www.tamaragill.com
tamaragillauthor@gmail.com

Manufactured by Amazon.ca
Bolton, ON